Katie's head jerked around. "You told me you never did this before."

"I said I never had to ditch, and that's true. I have had to make emergency landings before. It's all part of the job."

"Oh!" Katie heaved a sigh and felt her terror slipping away. "For a moment—I mean, I thought—so you've had your motor stop before. I was afraid it was the first time—"

Mark bit his lip, as if debating whether to speak. "It is," he confessed in a low voice. "I've never had the engine quit like this before. But it doesn't mean anything," he added quickly. "It's all the same. We're just landing without power, that's all. It's not much trickier."

Katie wasn't sure she believed him.

Heather didn't. She was still huddled in a tight ball, her doll wedged under her arm and her hands hiding her eyes. "We're crashing," she moaned.

"No, we're not," said Laurie. "Dad just said so."

"He's going to kill us like Mommy."

The plane lurched to the left, broadsided by a heavy gust of wind. Heather squealed and Mark gripped the controls more tightly. Sweat had beaded on his forehead and he was breathing hard through clenched teeth. Katie felt her stomach sink, both from the sudden jerk of the plane and from Heather's startling moan. *Kill us like Mommy?*

THE WINGS OF ADRIAN

Jan Seabaugh

Serenade/Serenata
BOOKS

of the Zondervan Publishing House
Grand Rapids, Michigan

A Note from the Author:
I love to hear from my readers! You may correspond with me by writing:

>Jan Seabaugh
>Author Relations
>1415 Lake Drive, S.E.
>Grand Rapids, MI 49506

THE WINGS OF ADRIAN
Copyright © 1986 by Jan Seabaugh

Serenade/Serenata is an imprint of Zondervan Publishing House,
1415 Lake Drive, S.E., Grand Rapids, MI 49506.

ISBN 0-310-47342-X

Scripture quotations are taken from the *Holy Bible: New International Version* (North American Edition), copyright © 1973, 1978, 1984, by the International Bible Society, used by permission of Zondervan Bible Publishers.

Edited by Lynda S. Parrish
Designed by Kim Koning

Printed in the United States of America

86 87 88 89 90 91 / ZO / 10 9 8 7 6 5 4 3 2 1

For my husband, Jake,
". . . the stuff of which dreams are made."

CHAPTER 1

THE FIRST TIME KATIE REED SAW the airplane, she knew it was going to crash. Her lifelong terror of flying washed through her, numbing her head and arms, turning her stomach, and leaving her legs quivering. She gulped for air and gripped her leather-bound Bible, trying frantically to think of a Scripture passage, *any* Scripture passage, that would promise her a safe trip. But her mind wouldn't work, and she clutched her Bible tightly against her heart.

She sat down quickly in the brown leather easy chair poised in front of the windows overlooking the runways. Although the lobby was air-conditioned, she was sweating in her navy blue suit jacket. Someone opened a door behind her, and a warm autumn breeze rushed into the lounge, catching the edges of her thick chestnut hair and blowing it across her face, a pretty face with dark brown eyes and an elegantly shaped mouth, a face that now looked pale and frightened.

"Lord Jesus," she whispered, "do I have to?"

Katie could see four other planes parked beside the one she was supposed to fly in, all of them tethered to the ground. They looked flimsy, like giant toys designed for hobby collecting or hanging from mobiles in a little boy's bedroom. They were not meant to carry living people miles above the ground.

A stiff breeze kicked across the runway. Her chartered plane rocked on its moorings, its blue and white body gleaming in the strong sunshine. Katie saw how easily it moved, this little single-engine Dakota that could fit inside her parents' living room. The only other time Katie had flown, she had taken a jumbo jet, and even though she had been just as terrified, she had at least felt as if she were in a real airplane. She had the assurance of four strong engines, a highly-trained flight crew, and enough sheer bulk to show up on a radar screen. This paper airplane was a mote of dust in comparison.

Katie's hand trailed over the leather case enclosing her Bible, her fingertip tracing the engraved letters of her name. If she, Katie Allison Reed, didn't have faith in the counsel of her dear friend Mary Grace Kimball, she would have picked up her suitcase and gone straight to the nearest phone booth to call a cab. But Mary Grace had never been wrong about what Katie needed, and she had insisted that her young friend go to the Glory Mountain Christian Singles Retreat this year.

Singles. Katie felt a salty lump forming in her throat and fresh tears threatening to sting her red-rimmed eyes. She fumbled in her purse for her sunglasses, wanting to hide the evidence of a week-long crying jag, but realized she hadn't brought them. Swallowing roughly and turning her back to the lobby, she again caught sight of the five airplanes parked outside. The familiar sensations of fear rushed through her body.

A door opened behind her. The window glass reflected a white-coated man entering the lobby, and for a moment her heart quickened. She peeked discreetly over her shoulder, hoping the impossible had happened and Steve had come to find her. She imagined him careening through midday traffic in his battered red Volkswagen, racing to the airport to keep his fiancée from flying away in a flimsy little airplane that had no business being in the air. She could see him skidding into a parking space, leaping from the car, and running up the steps to the lobby, his lab coat flying open, his stethoscope dangling from his neck, and his blue eyes searching every corner for his bride-to-be.

Ex-bride-to-be. And the man wasn't Steve. Tears smarted Katie's eyes. She felt irrationally angry, watching this intruder in a soiled white raincoat drop coins in the Pepsi machine and walk away sipping from a paper cup. The stranger did not suspect that he had contributed to the second worse day of Katie Reed's life. Even his ring, a thick gold class ring with a brilliant red stone, was identical to Steve's.

Katie faced the airplanes again, and her stomach fluttered. If that airplane didn't kill her, memories of Steve surely would.

Katie closed her eyes and thought about the past year, those wonderful, terrible days marching single file up to this paralyzing moment, and her throat went completely dry. One year and one day ago she had met Steve on a warm autumn afternoon, and she knew that, for the rest of her life, autumn would remind her of him.

She had met his ring first. It had come flying across the hallway, bounced off the rubber tree at the edge of the nurses' station, and landed at her feet. Katie had been so startled she had dropped purchase orders, scheduling forms, and administrative memos all over the floor. A moment later she met Steve, crawling on his hands and knees out of the door of 420, the room everyone else on Pediatrics had been tiptoeing around. Katie picked up the ring and stared at the man in the white coat scrambling around on the floor.

"Just what do you think you're doing?"

The man, rising up on his knees, spotted his ring in her hand. "Why don't you give me a ring sometime?" he said, grinning at the no-nonsense manager of the Pediatrics Unit from underneath unkempt blond hair.

A student nurse at the station tittered. Katie scowled and pointed toward Room 420. "There's a very sick little boy in there."

The man stood up, took his ring from her, and placed it on his finger. "I know, I'm his doctor." He touched his name tag, which read, *Steve Rose, M.D.*

Katie blushed, embarrassed because she had growled at a doctor and because the student nurse was laughing openly now.

"Excuse me." She bent to retrieve her papers. Dr. Steve Rose watched her tidy the stack and place them neatly on her desk, then reached over and took her hand.

"C'mon, manager," he said. "You look like you need a good game of ring-toss."

Katie spent the next fifteen minutes of her shift tossing Steve's ring at a blue plastic kidney bowl set on the floor of Room 420, taking turns with Philip and his doctor. Katie scored fifty points, watched the sick boy smile for the first time in two weeks, and fell in love with his doctor.

When the cardiac surgeon arrived, Katie went back to her desk and her papers, but she couldn't concentrate on anything but the occupants of Room 420. Both doctors emerged later while she was on the phone with the storeroom. As the elevator doors closed, she saw Steve pull off his ring, toss it in the air, and wave good-by to her.

An hour later, the orders for Philip's surgery came across her desk: it was scheduled for the next morning. Philip's mother arrived, pale and nervous, and the traffic in and out of 420 caused a round of frightened tears and tantrums.

Steve Rose showed up again, this time with a Monopoly game under his arm, and Katie didn't make it home that night. On her way to punch out, she wound up buying railroads and real estate, and landing on Boardwalk at the worst possible time. Philip fell asleep at two-thirty in the morning, while Dr. Rose, Philip's mother, and the Pediatrics Unit manager traded deeds and conversation all night. Philip was wheeled to surgery at seven, his mother headed for the blue upholstered lounge to wait, and Katie was treated to bacon and eggs before she fell asleep on the doctor's shoulder in the battered red Volkswagen he drove her home in.

For almost a year, Katie's life revolved around Steve's crazy hours. She ate breakfast at midnight, dinner at dawn, played tennis at night, and went bowling at noon. She waited long hours for him in the plush lounge of the office he shared with five other doctors, and in the cold, brown-tiled clinic where he volunteered time to sick children with tattered clothes and hungry eyes.

Steve's dream was to open a clinic of his own, where he could "make a difference . . . a real difference!" Katie knew she wanted to be right there at the front desk of that clinic, handling the paperwork, welcoming the patients, and helping Steve make that difference in their lives.

Steve had the same idea. During an impromptu noon-time picnic in June, he set up a game of ring-toss, using his shoe as the target. Katie tossed in his class ring and pulled out her diamond.

"A thousand points," said Steve. "Name your wedding day."

Katie's mother thought Steve was perfect. Katie's father called him "a fine young man." The nurses labeled Katie lucky, and Katie counted herself wonderfully blessed.

But Mary Grace Kimball folded her gnarled hands across her Bible and told Katie she was making a mistake.

"Yes, he's wonderful. Yes, he's a fine man. Yes, he's almost everything a woman could want. But is he a Christian?"

Katie ducked her head, unwilling to meet Mary Grace's eyes. "Almost," she said reluctantly.

"What's 'almost' a Christian, Katie? Is he or isn't he?"

"Not yet."

"Oh? Do you expect him to become one soon?"

"He could. He's such a dedicated doctor, and he loves children so much. A man with such a loving, compassionate heart could make a fine Christian, if he just had time to think about it and work into it slowly. . . ."

"Have you talked to him about the Lord?"

"A few times."

"And?"

11

"He's not very interested. But that'll change, Mary Grace."

Katie believed it. She felt that heavy ache in her heart that came from knowing her husband-to-be was not impressed by the most important thing in her life. She had prayed about it, asking God to work in Steve's heart. She quit asking him to go to church with her and stopped going to her own fellowship meetings, telling herself that if she didn't pressure him, he would take an interest naturally and be won over by her example. But it never seemed to be the right time. He handed back the books and pamphlets she offered him and kidded her out of every discussion she tried to start. With a lover's faith she told herself she could change him, once they were married.

Mary Grace was not convinced. "I've heard that one before, Katie Reed. Young women always overestimate their power over the men they love. They just know he'll stop drinking or gambling or hitting them, if they just love him enough. Hogwash! Don't you believe it."

"But the Bible says that faithful wives can win their husbands to the Lord."

"He's not your husband, Katie. That Scripture's not for you. Your text comes a little later." Mary Grace opened her Bible to 2 Corinthians. She traced her finger down the columns. "Here it is. 'Do not be yoked together with unbelievers.' That verse has your name on it. You've got no business marrying Steve Rose. It's an unequal yoke you're asking for, and you'll get hurt."

Even then Katie knew that Mary Grace was right, but she couldn't accept it. In Steve's arms the differences between them seemed trivial. But in the hours they were apart, those differences became a sword dangling over her head. Katie searched her Bible for the answer she wanted and prayed for signs that God approved of her wedding plans.

Mary Grace scowled at her. "What do you expect God to tell you that he hasn't already said? It's right here in the Word. Steve is an unbeliever. Don't do it, Katie. Don't."

Katie didn't listen. Her bridesmaids were fitted in rose-colored crepe gowns, while she squirmed in her heavy white satin and lace. Her headpiece was too tight, the veil lopsided. Katie's mother, wearing out under the strain of planning for two hundred guests, fussed and got headaches. Her father sighed over the cost and made jokes about eloping. Steve was sweet. "It's your day, Katie. Have it any way you want it."

Mary Grace shook her head. "Katie, don't do it."

It had ended one week ago today.

Katie's pastor called her at work. "I understand that your fiancé is a busy doctor, Katie," he said, "but you've cancelled three appointments for premarital counseling and it's only one week until your wedding. I've been patient about this, but if you want me to perform your wedding, I have to insist. I must see you both."

Steve was offended. "I'm a doctor," he complained. "I'm a trained medical professional. I don't need counseling. I know what I'm doing!"

"I know that, Steve, but he won't perform our wedding unless we come in and talk to him. It's one of his rules. He says he won't help people buy themselves a lifetime of unhappiness. . . ."

"I'm not offering you one."

"I know that, but he insisted. Please, Steve."

"If it's important to you . . ."

"It is."

Steve was twenty minutes late. He hurried into the pastor's office, his lab coat open, his stethoscope draped over his neck. He looked the portrait of the busy young doctor. Katie, embarrassed by his lateness, was still proud of him when he arrived.

Her pride plummeted within ten minutes. Ten terrible minutes.

"I owe it to you to be honest," Steve said in his reasonable voice. "I'm a very steady man. I have a good job, a good heart, and I do the best I can to get along with people. I love Katie, and I'm planning to be married to her happily for the rest of my life. But I don't buy all the

13

religious talk. I'm too much of a realist for that. I'm just not a person who believes in God."

The pastor had been as polite as he could, but he could not cushion Katie against his decision not to perform the wedding ceremony.

"It's no big deal," said Steve, over coffee later. "I'm sorry if you had your heart set on that church, but it's not the only one in town. Let's drive around until we find another one you like. There's bound to be someone who will marry us without any strings attached."

Katie remembered clearly the sick feeling in her stomach. "There's more at stake here than finding another church." For the first time she realized how carefully she had avoided facing the problem. "God is the center of my life. I can't go into my marriage . . . our marriage . . . without your feeling the same way."

"I thought I was the center of your life." Steve put down his cup and looked at her as if she were crazy.

"You're next."

"Oh, come on! I know you're really into the religious thing, but I thought you knew by now I wasn't. I didn't think we ever had to talk about it. You do your thing, and I'll do mine. Why can't we let it go at that?"

"Because we'd never really be together, Steve. Not the way God meant for a man and a woman to be."

"Do you know how sanctimonious you sound?"

Katie winced. She quickly put down her trembling cup before she dropped it. "I don't mean to, Steve, but you've got to give me a chance. If you would just listen to me . . . let me tell you what I've experienced with the Lord, maybe you—"

"No. Sorry, but no. I don't believe there is a God. All we really have is our minds and our hands and each other to make this world work. We can't waste time praying and looking for visions. The answer to life is in our own hands. This is real life, Katie, not some Easter movie."

Katie felt sick. Her hands turned cold all the way to her fingertips.

"You're as free as I am to believe anything you choose," Steve went on. "If you want to believe in some

14

kind of God, that's fine, as long as it works for you. I don't care. Maybe we should get married on neutral ground instead of in a church. There's still time to line up a hall."

"Steve, please listen . . ."

"I think you should. We were fine until we walked into that dead-end counseling session. If we hadn't done that, nothing would have changed. I'm the same. You're the same. Now, let's make new plans."

Katie would never forget the shocked and disgusted look on his face when she said no.

She had spent two days in bed, locked away from her mother's lectures and her father's questions. She was incapable of dealing with the humiliation of cancelling her wedding and returning her shower gifts. Everyone wanted to know why, and everyone kept asking if she would set another date. Her mother stoically responded that the wedding was definitely off. Only to her close friends did she confide that her daughter's fanaticism had cost her a fine son-in-law.

Mary Grace had come to her door on the third day, bringing a large box of tissues and a brochure about the Glory Mountain Christian Singles Retreat. Its theme this year, which Mary Grace had underlined three times in red ink, was "Trust God."

"He'll reward your faithfulness," she promised. "Trust him, Katie. Go to that retreat and immerse yourself in the Word. Put your mind on trusting God, and he'll take this pain away."

Katie let herself be swayed. She changed her vacation from her planned honeymoon dates to the dates of the retreat and called to make a train reservation, only to find that no train would take her close enough to Glory Mountain Lodge. She would have to drive or fly.

Flying was out of the question, so Katie made plans to drive. The day before the retreat her car died. Katie told herself she was not about to drive an unfamiliar car one hundred and fifty miles through steep, curving mountain roads.

"I can't go," she told Mary Grace that evening. "Thank you for trying to help, but—"

"But nothing, Katie Reed. Did you call the airlines?"

"Well, no, but—"

"Katie?"

"You know how I feel about flying!"

"If you can't trust the Lord to hold up an airplane, then you *really* need to go! You need a good booster shot of trust."

But Katie waited too long to call. No commercial flights could get her to Glory Mountain in time.

Mary Grace mused a while, sipping lemon-scented tea. She brightened up so suddenly she almost spilled it. "Of course you can go! My nephew and his family go fishing in that part of the Rockies, and they fly up in a private plane. That's it—we'll use his pilot and plant you right on the doorstep!"

Katie's mind spun, along with her stomach. "Fly? Fly? In one of those little things? Oh, Mary Grace, I can't!"

But Mary Grace was already dialing the phone. "If God wants you there, then he's already taken care of it. You go and pack, dear. And by the way, this is my un-wedding gift to you. This one's a pleasure to give!"

It seemed as if God didn't have the Glory Mountain Christian Singles Retreat in mind when he planned Katie's life. Mary Grace's nephew reported that his pilot was on a job up in Canada. Of the three other names of pilots he gave her to try, two were already busy. Mary Grace resolutely dialed the last phone number while Katie lingered in the doorway of her bedroom, dragging her feet about packing, hoping that this last one would be busy, too.

Mary Grace gave her the thumbs up. Katie winced and went in to pack.

"I knew the Lord would find you a pilot!" said Mary Grace. "You'll be leaving tomorrow at three o'clock, just in time to make the registration hour and dinner! And you'll be taxied to Glory Mountain in a plane called *Adrian*. Isn't that a lovely name?"

"I don't care about the name. Is it safe?"

"Katie, with you aboard, she'll be downright blessed."

Adrian didn't look blessed. She looked dangerous.

"If I rise on the wings of the dawn, if I settle on the far side of the sea, even there your hand will guide me. . . ." At last a Scripture text had come to Katie, but it gave her little comfort. Her beloved Psalm 139 was meant to be read at her wedding, not out here in a drafty lobby while a blue and white toy airplane grinned maliciously at her through the window.

Katie opened her Bible and turned to the psalm, letting her eyes drink in the comforting assurance of God's love and personal interest in her life. Katie usually felt relieved after reading this psalm, but today the promises made her feel uncomfortable.

The door to the lobby slammed open against the wall, rattling the Pepsi machine and startling the desk clerk. A man strode in, carrying a kicking, crying child under one arm and propelling a struggling teenaged girl with the other.

The older girl wrenched herself free and flounced on the chair across from Katie's. She was about thirteen, with straight blond hair pulled back in barrettes. She pulled her legs up onto the seat and folded her arms across her green sweatshirt, her lower lip stuck out in an angry pout.

The younger girl was about six. She kicked wildly at the man holding her and beat her curled fists against his back. "I don't want you! Put me down!" she shrieked.

The desk clerk came around the front of his desk. "Is there something I can do—?"

The man set the girl down and started to answer, but she wriggled past him and ran back toward the door. He dived after her and caught her around the waist, swinging her around roughly while she hit and kicked. "Let me go! Let me go!"

"Put her down!" snapped the older girl.

The man carried her over to the window, passing in front of Katie. The girl's flailing foot knocked Katie's Bible out of her hands onto the floor. He set the child down and knelt in front of her with a tight grip on her arms. "Now listen to me, Heather," he said. "This is a

17

dangerous place. You have to watch where you're going. Stay away from the airplanes. Go sit by your sister."

Heather stared at him, silent and hostile.

"You could walk into a propeller." The child squirmed out of his grasp and ran to the older girl, who gathered her into her arms and onto her lap. They both sat there, glaring at him.

Katie tried not to stare, but couldn't help herself. She was caught off guard by the tall man in front of her. Well-tanned and solidly built, he was dressed in a plaid hunting shirt, jeans, and boots; a knife rested in a sheath on his hip. His hair, dark brown with threads of silver, was longer than Katie liked, but its pioneer look suited him. A snatch of an old song ran through Katie's mind:

Raised in the woods so he knew every tree,
Kil't him a bar when he was only three . . .

Going over to the desk, he spoke with the clerk in low tones and began to complete a form, glancing at the girls every few seconds to make sure they didn't run off.

Katie reached for her Bible and froze when she heard the squeal of brakes.

Steve?

She twisted around. A middle-aged woman in a tweed suit barged through the door with her fists clenched and her red face set in a snarl. The girls squeaked, "Grandma!" and started to get up.

The man snapped his fingers and pointed a long finger at them. "Stay there!"

They shrank back into the brown leather cushions.

The woman stationed herself between their chair and the man. "You can't take them, Mark McLaren! You've got no right to these children now!"

"I've got every right!"

The desk clerk turned pale. "Is there a problem here. . . ?"

"No!" said Mark.

"Yes! Call the police! This man is kidnapping my granddaughters!"

The clerk's mouth dropped open. His hand hovered

18

above the telephone, but Mark pressed his own hand over the receiver, holding it down.

"You can't kidnap your own children," said Mark evenly.

"I've got a lawyer! I won't give them to you!"

"Then go talk to your lawyer. Get off my back!"

"You've got no right to them!"

"And you do? Show me something. Show me a piece of paper that says they're yours and not mine!"

The woman bristled. "I'll have one by the time you get back! I've got a lawyer! I won't let you have them!"

The desk clerk cleared his throat. "Perhaps you should delay your flight until this is settled—"

"It *is* settled." Mark scrawled his signature across the bottom of the form and pushed it across the desk.

The woman dropped her hands to her sides, heaving a sigh. She turned to the girls and placed her hands on their shiny blond hair.

"Don't worry. This is the last time you'll ever have to see him. As soon as he brings you back I'll have him in court and everything will be all right. I promise."

"Don't make me go!" cried Heather.

"It'll be all right," the grandmother said, throwing an ugly look over her shoulder at Mark. "Just try to put up with it." She hugged them both and turned on Mark, her fist in the air. "This isn't over, Mark McLaren! I'll never let you take them away from me again!"

Mark watched his daughters say good-by to her, and although he was still flushed with anger, Katie thought she detected a flash of hurt and sadness in his deep hazel eyes. When the grandmother left, he looked apprehensive. He wiped his forehead with his hand, trying to calm himself down. Then he noticed Katie.

Katie felt awkward, caught in the middle of a family quarrel. She picked up her Bible and wished her pilot would show up and take her out of here.

Mark looked her over thoroughly, taking in the details of her navy blue suit, white bowed blouse, and black leather pumps. He focused on the white suitcase by the side of her chair, then fished in his pocket and pulled out a small notebook.

19

"Are you Katie Reed?"

Her stomach turned. It couldn't be.

"You're not my pilot, are you?"

He nodded. "I'm Mark McLaren. Those are my daughters—" He gestured toward them. "Laurie's the older one, and the little one is Heather."

"Are they going too?" Katie knew the answer already. She didn't want to go anywhere with this volatile, squabbling family.

"They sure are."

"Is that allowed?" She looked appealingly at the desk clerk, who nodded apologetically and got busy with his papers. "I mean, I thought I was supposed to have a professional pilot."

"You are, and I am. I'm a flight instructor, too, if that makes you feel any better."

"But this is a chartered flight. You're not supposed to bring your children along."

"You're the cargo on this trip, Miss Reed. I'm diverting from my flight plan to drop you off at Endicott Field. After that, we're going camping for a week on the other side of Glacier Park."

Heather folded her arms defiantly. "I don't want to go!"

Mark ignored her. "You still want to come along?"

Katie debated quickly. This was her chance to bail out. She almost said no, but Mary Grace's kind, firm face swam before her. Mary Grace had never been wrong about what Katie needed.

"Yes, I'm coming," she finally replied. "I hope I won't be in the way."

"You *are* the way, Miss Reed. You're paying for this trip. I had to buy all new gear for the girls—decent sleeping bags, down vests, and a new tent. They still don't have proper shoes for the mountains but I didn't know what sizes to get."

"I like my own shoes!" pouted Heather.

"All that costs money, so don't back out on me, Miss Reed. It's only a ninety-minute trip."

"I won't."

He gave her another long look, and she felt herself turning red again. "I'll take your bag. I've got preflight checks to make, but we'll be taking off in about fifteen minutes."

"Taking off!" Katie's old terror blitzed back.

Mark grinned. "You're afraid of flying, aren't you?"

"Why would you think that?"

"You look like you're about to pass out. Try not to worry. I've never ditched a plane yet. We'll make it."

"Thank you. I needed that." Katie tried to smile, but failed.

"Where are you going?"

Katie's eyes widened. "Don't you know?"

Mark laughed. "Take it easy. I know where to fly you to. I'm asking where you're going from there. I'd bet my plane you're not going to vacation on the edge of a landing field."

"Oh. I'm going on a retreat at Glory Mountain Lodge."

Mark's grin collapsed. "You're one of those."

Katie was jarred by his sudden mood shift. "If you mean a Christian, then you're right."

He was staring at the Bible in her hand. "Look, Reed, it's ninety minutes to Endicott Field. You think you can keep your mouth shut that long? If you can't, find another plane. And keep that Bible out of my sight. Sit on it, if you have to, but don't open it or you'll be walking to Glory Mountain." He picked up her bag and strode out the door toward the planes.

Stunned, Katie stole an embarrassed look at the girls. They stared back stonily.

"Is he always like this?"

Laurie shrugged. "How should I know? We haven't seen him for a year."

CHAPTER 2

KATIE STOOD AWKWARDLY by a chain link fence outside
the lounge, twisting the strap of her white shoulder bag.
Mark was walking slowly around the *Adrian,* removing
the mooring lines, checking the oil level, inspecting the
tires, and examining the propeller with practiced hands.
He carried a small manual with him and referred to it
every minute or so. Katie swallowed and glanced over at
Laurie, who was sitting Indian style on the asphalt with
her arm around her little sister.

"Why does he keep looking at that book?" Katie tried
not to sound as nervous as she felt. "Doesn't he know
what to do without a list?"

"Pilots always use a checklist," said Laurie. "It's
standard procedure."

Katie was relieved, not wanting to believe the man
didn't know how to fly his own airplane. "Have you
flown in that plane before?"

"Sure, lots of times. He used to take me camping with
him all the time." Katie thought she detected pride in
Laurie's voice, but she wasn't sure.

Heather scowled up at her sister. "How come he took
you and not me?"

"You were too little. Mom wouldn't let him take you

22

without her and she only came once and hated it. She never came again.''

Heather wasn't satisfied with that answer. She stuck out her lower lip. "He never took me.''

Katie watched Mark secure the baggage compartment door. She thought of her white suitcase locked inside and felt a sensation of panic. She was now committed to the flight since she couldn't grab her bag and run.

"I'm going to hate it,'' Heather announced.

"It's not so bad,'' said Laurie. "You'll get to fish and use a sleeping bag. You might even see some deer running around. They're beautiful in the wild.''

"It sounds like fun,'' said Katie.

"It used to be.''

"You'll probably have a wonderful time after you drop me off.''

"No, we won't,'' said Heather. "There's going to be bugs and snakes and bears and dirt all over the place. I hate camping.''

Katie knew she would feel the same way if she were going to the wilds instead of a warm lodge with all the modern conveniences. "How do you know you'll hate it? You've never been camping in your life. Maybe you'll love it.''

"Uh-uh!'' denied Heather. "Grandma said we'd hate it. She said we'd get cold and probably catch pneumonia and it would be all his fault. And she said it's all just a trick to try to get us back, but it won't work. We're not going back to him. Not ever!'' She looked at Laurie for approval. "Right?''

"Right,'' said Laurie dully, her eyes on her father. She reached over and put her arm around Heather again.

Katie looked back and forth between them, curious to know what Heather meant but not wanting to pry. The sunlight blazed down and glinted off their blond hair, so unlike their father's dark hair. She glanced over at Mark and saw no resemblance at all. "You two must look like your mother.''

"Mommy was beautiful,'' said Heather. "Grandma said she looked like Sleeping Beauty in my storybook.''

23

"I remember that story. I always liked the part when the prince kisses her and breaks the evil spell."

Heather's face froze. Tears welled up in her eyes and spilled over onto her cheeks. She opened her mouth and let out a low, dismal sob, then twisted around to hide her face against Laurie's shoulder.

Katie was taken aback by the sudden display of sorrow.

"I'm sorry," she said quickly, wondering what had triggered it.

Laurie didn't seem to know either. "Heather," she urged, "come on, it's okay. Don't cry anymore." But Heather responded only with more muffled sobs. Laurie looked up at Katie helplessly. "I don't know what made her do that."

"Maybe I shouldn't have said anything about your mother."

"Oh, no," said Laurie eagerly. "I like to talk about Mom. Grandma does too, but it's always stuff about when Mom was a little girl. She doesn't know much about the things I remember, when Mom was painting me."

Katie sensed the girl's need to talk but felt torn by Heather's grief. She felt an urge to take the child into her own arms and soothe her, but it was too intimate a gesture for a stranger. "Was your mother a painter?" she asked, hoping she wouldn't set Heather off again.

"She was an artist," corrected Laurie. "There's a picture of me over Grandma's fireplace that Mom painted when I was two. I remember posing for it, even though Mom said I was too little to remember. She always wore a white smock over her clothes and played music on the stereo. I want to be an artist someday, just like she was, only I'm going to paint the outdoors. I like deer. Someday I'm going to do a big painting of wild deer in the mountains and hang it over my own fireplace, when I have a house."

"Was your mother's name Adrian?"

Heather stopped crying and stared up at her. "How did you know?"

"Just a guess. I saw the name on the airplane, and—"

"The plane!" Heather jumped up and ran a few steps toward the blue and white Dakota. She saw the gleaming blue letters against the white bow and pointed. "Make him take it off! Make him take her name off his airplane!"

Mark looked up from his flight manual. "What's going on over there?" he growled, glaring at Katie as if it were her fault.

Laurie looked away, leaving Katie to answer him alone. "There's nothing wrong," she said uncertainly. "Heather's a little upset over the name of your airplane, that's all."

Mark slammed the manual shut. "What do you want me to call it? The 'Katie Reed'?"

"Now, wait a minute! I don't care what you call your plane. It's your daughter who's upset over it, not me."

"Well, they're coming along whether you like it or not. If you don't like it, pray for a lousy chariot of fire to fly you up to Glory Mountain."

The biblical reference startled Katie, but his insolent tone made her angry. She fought it down.

Mark tossed the manual into the cabin of the plane and jerked his thumb toward the door. "It's time to leave. Everybody in."

"I don't want to go," said Heather, "and you take Mom's name off your dumb airplane!"

Mark was over to her in two strides. He grabbed her and swung her, kicking, into the air and deposited her on the wing. "Up front, Heather."

"I'm not sitting next to you!"

"Then get in the back. Put your seat belt on. Laurie, let's go."

"I want to sit beside Heather."

"What a surprise." He gestured toward the rear seats. "Make sure those belts are on good and tight." He reached out to help her but Laurie snapped away from his touch and climbed in unaided.

Mark looked impatiently at Katie. "That leaves you, Reed. Sorry, but you're stuck up front with me." He glowered at the Bible in her hands. "That can go in the back with your luggage."

"I'd rather keep it with me."

"That's right, you're scared of flying. Well, if we get into trouble, don't expect that to help you unless you've got a parachute folded up inside it."

Katie bit back her urge to retort. She approached the plane cautiously, and in an instant her anger with Mark McLaren dissolved in the realization that the time had come. Her stomach flip-flopped and she breathed in sharply. She couldn't make herself move.

"Come on, Reed," Mark said shortly, and he climbed up on the wing. He paused to look back at her, and his expression softened. "Do you need some help?"

"I've—I've never flown in a little plane before, and—"

"Here." He pointed at a handhold on the side of the plane. "Take hold of that, and step up on the wing."

He reached out for her hand and pulled her gently onto the wing, then took hold of her arm to steady her. He propelled her up toward the cabin door. Katie almost dropped her Bible, then found herself sitting in a blue upholstered seat staring at the runway before her. The propeller stuck up in front of the windshield. She squared her shoulders, determined not to look as frightened as she felt. It was suddenly very important that Mark McLaren not think she was a coward.

"I'm fine," she said aloud. "Thank you."

"That's great," he answered. "Now let go of my arm."

She realized her nails were digging into his sleeve. She let go quickly, aware of a giggle from the girls, and she felt herself blushing. It was a strange sensation, because she wasn't embarrassed by her fear of flying. The blush had another cause, her sudden, emotional response to Mark McLaren's touch. It had caught her off guard, and as she let go of him she felt an alien urge to reach out and take hold of him again.

Mark folded up his six-foot, three-inch frame to get through the narrow cabin door without bumping his head, and squeezed past Katie's knees to drop into the pilot's seat on the left. He reached across her to close and lock the door.

She caught a faint aroma of coffee and gingersnaps when he reached across her, and she felt a twinge of hunger. She had hardly eaten a thing all week since her terrible scene with Steve.

She watched Mark's hands moving expertly over the controls. The instrument panel was large and complicated, a riot of dials and gauges that gleamed in the sun and made Katie dizzy. There were two U-shaped steering wheels, one of them jutting out over Katie's lap. She touched it delicately.

"Don't worry, I won't make you drive," said Mark, flipping switches and dials with assured ease. "This is the fuel selector valve. We'll fly the first hour on one tank, then switch to the other and run it dry, then switch back to the first tank."

"Why do you do that?"

"To keep the plane in lateral trim."

"What?"

"Balanced. You don't want us to tip over in the air, do you?"

Katie gulped. "Could we?"

"Haven't you ever seen stunt planes turning somersaults?"

"We're not going to do that!"

Mark chuckled. "It might be fun, Reed. It would give you something to tell your grandchildren."

"Please don't do anything tricky." She studied the incomprehensible panel. "How can you watch all these things at once?"

"I watch the ones I have to watch. Some of the others are radios. There are eleven different radios in this plane. Did you know that?"

Katie shook her head. "I've only seen those movies where there's only one radio, and it quits at the worst possible time."

"That's purely show biz. We'd have to crack up the front end of the plane to knock all those radios out." He opened a paperback manual and handed it to her. "Here. You can follow along and see what I'm doing." He opened the throttle a little bit, turned on a switch that the manual said was the master switch, then started the electric fuel pump. He reached for the starter, pausing until Katie located it on the schematic in the book. "What's this?"

"The starter?"

The engine fired abruptly in reply and the propeller began to spin. Katie grasped her Bible tightly in one hand and the flight manual in the other, breathing a quick prayer for a safe flight.

"I don't want to go," complained Heather from the seat behind Katie.

"It's too late now." He opened the throttle fully. "Kiss the city good-by and get ready to rough it."

"I don't want to rough it," muttered Heather. She cuddled her doll, but Katie heard her breathing become quick and shallow and heard the undertone of fear in her defiant little voice. Katie felt sorry for the child, especially since she seemed to be as frightened of the airplane as Katie was.

"Are we taking off now?" asked Katie.

"Not yet. I have a ground check to make." Mark noted gauge readings and switched the fuel pump off for a moment. He told her he did that to make sure the engine-driven pump was operating, but Katie wasn't sure what he meant. She felt a flush of gratitude that he knew what he was doing. He ran through several checks, then said, "Is your door latched?"

"Yes." Katie turned to stare at the door. "It can't come open, can it?"

"Not unless you try to bail out."

The plane began to move forward, accelerating rapidly to 60 miles per hour. Katie felt her stomach sink and she braced herself against the seat, dropping the manual to clutch her Bible.

"When do we take off?" she asked, eyes closed.

"We already did. Take a look."

Katie opened her eyes and looked down at the little

airfield ebbing away below them. She felt a sensation of thrust against her midriff as the Dakota climbed. It seemed like hours passed before she felt the plane leveling off, although she knew it had only been minutes. She heard Heather whisper to her doll not to be afraid.

"Well, did you survive it?" asked Mark.

"It was nothing," announced Heather. Katie heard a page flip and knew Laurie was already absorbed in her mystery book, and she envied the girl's experience and lack of concern. Katie twisted around and saw that Heather was huddled in her seat, her eyes wide and moist. Katie impulsively reached back and took her hand.

"Are you all right, honey?"

Heather looked surprised, then grateful. She squeezed Katie's hand in return. "Sure, we're fine."

Forgetting Mark's earlier warning, Katie settled back in her seat and opened her Bible, but instead of reading she flipped aimlessly through the New Testament, her thoughts elsewhere. Mark had stopped talking to her now that the ordeal of the take-off was over with. She smiled to herself and tried to concentrate on God's promise that he would cause all things to work together for good for her, wondering how he could possibly put a broken engagement and a trip in a flimsy private airplane together for her good.

The pain of losing Steve seemed to recede as the plane banked and turned, and she watched Mark's strong hands guide the plane and thought how strange it was that she felt so safe. She drifted into daydreams of Mark taking her hand and helping her onto the wing of the plane, and little stabs of excitement pricked her as the warmth of her blush returned.

How stupid, she thought suddenly. *How absolutely stupid to go from thoughts of one wrong man to thoughts of another wrong man*. She felt foolish and angry with herself both at once. "Katie Allison Reed, get your head out of the clouds and get your mind on the Lord," she told herself fiercely.

"What are you doing, rehearsing?"

"I'm sorry—what?"

"You're talking to yourself. Are you getting ready to start?"

"Start what?"

"The Big Witness. Isn't that what you're gearing up for? There you sit, with your Bible open, mumbling under your breath. Did you figure I'd be a captive audience up here for two hours?"

"I wasn't thinking about you at all."

"Sure, you weren't. I know your kind. You all have that unholy drive to bring in the sheaves."

"I wouldn't call it *un*holy, Mr. McLaren."

"Excuse me, bad choice of words. But isn't it pounded into your head to go out and recruit every chance you get?"

"No one pounded anything into me. It's natural to want to spread the Good News."

"You've got some?"

"Of course I have. I've experienced something so wonderful, so life-changing, that I want to share it with other people."

"That's what I thought. Well, don't do it. You'll find out real quick that all that religious talk doesn't cut any ice with me, Reed."

"You brought it up. Maybe you've got a secret desire to hear about Jesus."

It was as though she had slapped him. Mark's face turned red and he radiated such anger she thought she could feel its heat against her face. "Watch it, Reed! I don't have any secret desires to hear all that garbage again! Maybe you've got some sick, psycho need to hang onto all that false hope, but when you really need help, you'll find out fast that you're all alone. There's no one out there to hear you, and the sooner you figure that out the better off you'll be!"

Katie blinked. For a moment it sounded as if she were talking with Steve again. The blast of hostility reminded her of her recent heartbreak, and the sensations of loss and humiliation swept unbidden through her heart. She struggled to hold them in check.

30

"That's not so, Mr. McLaren. I've been in a lot of need, and God has never forsaken me."

"I'm too realistic to believe that."

Realistic. One of Steve's words. Katie was annoyed by the power they still had over her. Mary Grace had been right to insist she get away and get her mind back on God.

"Besides," continued Mark, "Christians drive me up a wall. I can't stand people who keep their heads buried in the sand. I can't stand people who go around spreading the lie that there's a God up there who cares what happens to us down here."

Katie thought she heard a slight change of tone, a longing behind the explosion of anger, a forlorn cry for help masked by a show of disgust. "Mr. McLaren, could I tell you something about my own life?"

"Let me guess. It's your lightning-bolt conversion story, right?"

"It wasn't like that. . . ."

"We've got over an hour to kill. Go ahead, shoot."

Katie took a deep breath. "There was a time when I felt the same way you feel now. I thought Christians were silly and stuffy, and I didn't believe all the things I had been taught in Sunday school when I was a child. But when I got to college I started to have some trouble, and—"

"Did you get pregnant?"

Katie's eyes opened wide. "No! I—"

"Was it booze? Or were you into drugs?"

"I was confused about life," Katie began.

Mark laughed in a heavy burst. "Oh, Reed, we're all confused about life. Some of us run away from it and wind up fried on drugs or sloshed on booze. Some of us grab a Bible and claim we've caught rainbows. What's the difference what you do? It's all fantasy, and it's all weak."

Katie's head began to throb. He sounded more like Steve all the time. "The Lord is real, Mr. McLaren. Coming to him isn't being weak, it's becoming strong. When you give him control over your life—"

31

"Oh, stop it, Reed. I should've known better than to let you get started."

"You asked me," Katie pointed out.

"Just look out the window and fantasize or pray or do whatever it is you people do. Just keep quiet until we land, okay?"

Katie didn't know what to do. Part of her wanted to continue the conversation, shining light into all Mark McLaren's dark corners, but the other part of her felt pinned against the seat. She realized how half-hearted and automatic her witnessing had sounded, a proclamation of the goodness of a God who had just wrecked her life by coming between her and the man she had wanted to marry.

Katie closed her Bible and felt hot tears stinging her eyes.

What a terrible example she really was, trying to talk about the Lord to a man as worldly and experienced as this strong, rugged pilot who had probably known pain she couldn't begin to imagine. She suddenly felt insignificant and small. She listened to the steady hum of the plane's single engine, feeling its vibrations engulf her. She closed her eyes.

I'm sorry, Lord, I really blew it. I probably set you back a couple of years in trying to win Mark McLaren, by making my faith in you seem weak and silly. But it says in your Word that sometimes one plants a seed, another waters it, and another reaps. Well, I don't think I helped much, but you can send him someone who can. Please do that, Lord. Please send him someone who can really show him who you are. And Lord, please send me someone like that, too.

Katie felt her thumb pressed in her Bible. She opened it discreetly, conscious of Mark and peeked inside the leather-bound pages.

The first thing she saw was the name of the book of Mark, and as her eye skimmed the page she came to rest on the words, "At once the Spirit sent him out into the desert . . ."

The plane lurched. The sound of the engine changed, fading and thumping.

32

Katie gasped and turned to Mark. He calmly switched to another fuel tank.

"No problem," he announced.

Then the engine died.

Katie hugged her Bible tightly and the girls stared at their father in fright, wide-eyed with fright.

CHAPTER 3

HEATHER AND LAURIE SCREAMED at the same time. Katie's cry caught in her throat and for a moment she felt as if she were going to choke. She saw the astounded look on Mark's face and noticed he was switching back and forth between fuel tanks.

Laurie's voice shrilled from behind her, "Dad! The motor stopped!"

Mark jerked his head, as if to clear away the shock. "It's okay," he said quickly. "Don't anybody panic."

"It's not okay! The motor stopped!" screeched Laurie.

"We're crashing!" screamed Heather. She covered her face with her hands and rocked wildly from side to side. "We're crashing!"

"We're not going to crash," said Mark firmly. "I'm still in control of this plane. Now everybody calm down."

Katie realized she was holding her breath. She let it out so hard her chest heaved. "Can you start the motor again?"

Mark shook his head. "Not up here. I'm going to have to set it down."

"Set it down?" Katie stared out the window. Below

her the jagged peaks of the Rockies jutted up like daggers. "Set it down where? There's nothing down there but mountains!"

"There are lots of things down there besides mountains, Reed. We've got time to find a clear space somewhere."

"How much time?" Katie was sure the mountains were closer than they had been a moment before.

"I don't know. However long we can glide. A few minutes, at least." Mark reached for the radio. Heather sobbed loudly, drowning out Mark's voice as he spoke into the microphone. All Katie could make out was the cold, paralyzing word, "Mayday."

"Are we going to make it?" asked Laurie. Katie glanced back and saw Laurie's enormous green eyes dwarfing her pale face. "Tell me the truth, Dad. I want to know the truth."

Mark recited a list of numbers into the microphone, then raised his thumb. "No problem, sweetheart. I've done this lots of times."

Katie's head jerked around. "You told me you never did!"

"I said I never had to ditch, and that's true. I have had to make emergency landings before. It's all part of the job."

"Oh!" Katie heaved a sigh and felt her terror slipping away. "For a moment—I mean, I thought—so you've had your motor stop before. I was afraid it was the first time—"

Mark bit his lip, as if debating whether to speak. "It is," he confessed in a low voice. "I've never had the engine quit like this before. But it doesn't mean anything," he added quickly. "It's all the same. We're just landing without power, that's all. It's not much trickier."

Katie wasn't sure she believed him.

Heather didn't. She was still huddled in a tight ball, her doll wedged under her arm and her hands hiding her eyes. "We're crashing," she moaned.

"No we're not," said Laurie. "Dad just said so."

"He's going to kill us like Mommy."

35

The plane lurched to the left, broadsided by a heavy gust of wind. Heather squealed and Mark gripped the controls more tightly. Sweat had beaded on his forehead and he was breathing hard through clenched teeth. Katie felt her stomach sink, both from the sudden jerk of the plane and from Heather's startling moan. *Kill us like Mommy?* Katie struggled to catch her breath. Had Adrian McLaren died in a plane like this one, with her husband at the controls?

"Dad!" cried Laurie.

"It's nothing, sweetheart. Just the wind. We're still all right."

"How long will we be all right?" asked Katie. "Can the wind hurt us with the motor off?"

"It's making things a little tougher, that's all. I've flown in storms before." He grinned suddenly. "It looks like you're getting your money's worth, Reed. Transportation *and* excitement."

"Do you see a place to land yet?"

"Not yet."

"What if you can't?"

"I'll find a lake and ditch in the water."

"I didn't know you could do that in a plane like this. Aren't you supposed to have water skis on the bottom?"

"You mean floats. I didn't say we'd land, I said we'd ditch."

Katie's heart turned cold. "You mean, we'd crash."

"It's not the same thing. I'm in control. Don't forget that. I'm in control."

Laurie leaned forward and grabbed Mark's shoulder. "Dad! Heather can't swim!"

Mark glanced at Katie. "Can you?"

She shook her head. "Not for very long."

He bit his lower lip and thought. "Okay, the lake will be our last resort."

"What else is there?" asked Laurie raggedly.

"Treetops. If we can't find a level surface, we can land in the treetops."

"That's crashing!" cried Heather.

"No, it isn't. Not if you do it right. By the time we slip

down through all the branches, our impact will be nothing but a little bump. You won't even feel it."

Katie remembered being told that before getting a shot, and the shot had hurt anyway. For an instant she felt annoyed, being spoken to like a child, but the sight of the looming violet mountains jerked her out of annoyance back into alarm.

"If that's true," she said, "then it sounds good to me."

"Of course it's true." Mark's voice took on a hard edge. "Lying doesn't happen to be on my list of sins, lady."

"I'm sorry," she gulped. "Are we going to do that, then? Are we going for the treetops?"

"It's our next-to-the-last resort."

"But you said it wasn't dangerous—"

"I didn't say that, Reed. Anyway, it's harder to spot a downed aircraft when the view is blocked by trees. I want us out in the open where we're obvious."

"You mean, when all the rescue planes come?"

"*All* of them? Are you expecting the whole U.S. Air Force to turn out for us?" He frowned at her Bible. "You must think you've got a lot of influence."

Katie locked her sweating hands together to keep them still. "Just get us down—please!"

"My plan exactly."

The plane shuddered violently in the wind. Heather sobbed softly from behind her hands. "I don't want to die!"

"You're not going to," said Mark. "This plane is under control. Do I have to shout?"

Katie clutched her Bible tightly. "Yes," she said softly. "It is under control."

"Don't get religious on me, Reed. I meant *I'm* in control."

Katie closed her eyes. She tried to concentrate, tried to pray, but numbing fear blocked her. She wanted to feel the peace of God, that amazing peace that passed all understanding, but it wasn't there, just as it hadn't been there when she had decided not to marry Steve. All her

37

hurt and humiliation came back in a rush, turning her cold to her fingertips, and she gritted her teeth against the fresh terror of Mark's voice repeating that awful word, "Mayday."

"Help me," she whispered. "I can't find you."

"The mountains are closer," Laurie said. "We're going down!"

Mark nodded. "We're supposed to. We can't land if we're a mile up in the air, can we?"

"Land where? Dad, there isn't any place down there!"

Mark didn't answer. Heather's sobs began to sound hysterical. "Hold on to your sister," he told Laurie. "Try to calm her down."

Laurie moved back into her seat and slid her arms around Heather. "Don't worry," she said soothingly. "Dad's never crashed a plane yet."

Katie thought she detected a note of pride in Laurie's voice, a strange quality that didn't fit with the hostility the girl had expressed for him up to now. Her mind raced; if Mark McLaren had never crashed, then Adrian McLaren couldn't have died in a plane he was flying. Heather's cryptic comment taunted Katie, and she felt an overwhelming need to know everything about this odd little family and the shadow that hung over their lives.

The plane shook violently. Katie peeked out the window and was jolted by how close the treetops were.

"Are you going to land in the trees?" she asked.

"Looks that way. We've just about run out of time." Mark wiped his forehead, then squinted abruptly. His hands relaxed on the steering wheel and he laughed aloud. "No, I take it back. I'm going to land right there! Right there on that wonderful strip of level ground!"

"Where?" asked Laurie, scooting up again. "Where is it?"

"Two o'clock."

Laurie searched, then sighed loudly. "It is!"

"Oh, thank God," whispered Katie.

"Don't do that until we get down," said Mark coldly. He guided the plane to the right, bringing the landing site to his left. He banked slightly, beginning to spiral.

"Are you landing now?" asked Katie anxiously.

"Not yet. I've got to slow us down and make sure we're heading into the wind when we touch down. The less speed, the better."

"What if you do it too fast?"

"I won't."

Heather was calming down. "Are we really going to be all right?"

"We sure are, sweetheart," said Mark.

"I was talking to Laurie, not you!"

Katie saw him wince. He reached for the microphone again. "Make sure your seat belts are on tight," he ordered. He replaced the microphone and began to unbutton his plaid hunting shirt. "Help me get this off," he commanded.

Katie reached over and pulled the shirt off his broad back. It caught at the cuffs; Katie stretched her hands over his lap to undo the buttons so he wouldn't have to let go of the controls. She tugged the sleeves over his muscled arms, suddenly aware of how strong and tanned he looked in his white T-shirt. It was a silly thought and she thrust it out of her mind at once.

"Laurie, fold up my shirt and give it to Heather. Heather, when I tell you to, you put it over your face and bend forward."

"What for?" cried Heather, frightened again.

"So you won't bump your nose, baby."

"Don't call me that!"

"Yes, ma'am."

Laurie's fingers dug into his shoulder. "Crash positions?"

"It's nothing but standard operating procedure. Remember, we do everything by the book."

Katie removed her navy suit jacket. She passed it back to Laurie. "This is for you," she said, hoping her voice didn't sound as weak and thready as she thought it did.

"Thanks," said Laurie and Mark together.

The plane continued to spiral down in a carefully controlled fall. Mark's knuckles were pale from the effort of gripping the wheel, and Katie wondered whether he

39

was having trouble controlling the plane or if he was just as frightened as she was. The wind hit the plane straight on and Katie felt it tip more steeply to the left.

"Was that you or the wind?" she asked Mark in a whisper.

"The wind. I fly better than that."

"Are we still all right?"

"That might be a little exaggerated."

Katie felt sweat running down her face and arms. Her white blouse stuck to her and she plucked at it nervously. She tried once again to pray, and was shocked to realize she didn't know how. After three years of intense devotion to her Christian faith, she had no idea how to pray in a crisis. The feebleness of her faith sent painful pangs through her heart. "Please," she breathed, "let us land safely. Please . . ."

"Take your skirt off."

Katie jerked. "What?"

"Take your skirt off and protect your face. We're going to set down. Lean forward as far as you can."

Katie obeyed numbly, yanking down the zipper and sliding the gabardine skirt over her hips. She was grateful she still wore slips, even on hot days like this, thanks to her mother's proper training. She folded the skirt quickly and started to lean forward, but Mark stopped her. "The microphone," he said quickly. "I can't let go now."

Katie reached for it and switched the radio on as she had seen him do. He repeated coordinates a third time, mechanically but with a trace of fear in his voice that caused Katie to shudder.

"Everybody lean forward!" he said suddenly. "Cushions up!"

Katie buried her face in her wadded-up skirt and let the microphone drop.

There was no sensation. They were hanging in the air, motionless. Then the plane hit the ground so hard Katie felt the shock in every nerve and muscle of her body. The plane bounced once, twice, then rolled forward erratically, plowing the landing gear through the soft, moist ground. The tail flew up and the little Dakota pitched forward. Katie heard the horrible ripping sound as the left wing slammed into the earth, and an instant later the *Adrian* came to rest at a crazy angle, standing up on her nose.

"Everybody out!" shouted Mark. He reached over and tore open Katie's seat belt, and she grabbed the edges of her seat to keep from falling onto the floor. He leaned over the seat and yanked open Laurie's belt, but Heather's wouldn't budge. He unsnapped the sheath on his hip and pulled out a black-handled Buck knife.

He sawed rapidly through the webbed fabric while Heather screeched in terror, "Get me out! Get me out!"

Mark freed Heather from the belt and leaned across Katie. He kicked open the cabin door and dragged himself up through it. Heather scrambled over the seat, her arms groping above her, and Mark hauled her out across Katie's lap.

"Go on! Get out!" shouted Laurie.

Mark gripped Katie's arm and pulled her out. She fought to gain her balance, with her Bible in one hand, but the wing was tipped too steeply and she fell back against Mark.

"Down! Down!" he shouted in her ear, and pushed her off.

Katie caught a glimpse of Heather's shining blond hair and Mark's plaid hunting shirt, then gasped as she hit the ground and pain spiralled up her legs. She fell forward onto her knees.

"Run away from the plane!"

Katie didn't have to ask why. The defective engine could explode into flames behind them. Laurie hit the ground behind her and Katie struggled to her feet, searching for Heather. Somehow she had the child's hand in her own and all three jogged clumsily on aching legs over rocks and tufts of grass until they were on the edge of the tree line. Mark followed. There they waited, eyes fixed on the *Adrian,* waiting to see whether she would burn.

Nothing happened.

Laurie sank to the ground, her knees unable to support her any longer. Katie automatically knelt beside her and put her arms around her, and felt the answering pressure of Laurie's arms snaking around her waist. It was impossible to tell which of them was shaking harder.

Mark was the first to get up, studying the crumpled heap that had been his plane. "You stay here," he said. "I'm going to go and try to get our gear out."

"Isn't that dangerous?" asked Katie. "Couldn't it blow up?"

"It's not going to explode if it hasn't blown by now," he said. "Besides, you don't want all the rescue planes to find you looking like that, do you?"

Katie remembered she was in her blouse and slip and flushed. Mark picked his way carefully over the rough, soft ground and approached the plane cautiously. Katie couldn't help admiring the strength he radiated, the capability she sensed in him. Mark McLaren was a man who could take care of things. He was a man who could take care of them all. Even Katie Reed.

Katie began to feel exasperated with her own runaway emotions. This was certainly not the time to develop a crush, and especially not on such an insensitive, mocking man as Mark McLaren.

"Miss Reed," said Laurie weakly, "there's something wrong with Heather."

Katie turned to the child. Heather was up on her feet, staggering around aimlessly, struggling for balance. Her eyes were fixed and unfocused, like her doll's glassy eyes, and droplets of sweat had formed across her forehead and began to run down her cheeks. She was pale and trembling all over. Katie ran over to Heather and gripped her arms, startled by how cool and moist Heather's skin was.

"Heather? Heather, stop walking," Katie ordered softly. "Sit down, honey."

Heather looked at her blankly. Katie drew her down and held her tightly, suddenly helpless to know what to do. She tried to remember her first-aid training from college, but her mind couldn't come up with an answer.

42

She kept visualizing the jagged mountains and white knuckles gripping the steering wheel. She fought harder to recall first-aid procedure and thought of her Bible. What was she supposed to do? Praise him in all things? What did that have to do with this little child's odd behavior? Katie realized that she hadn't given thanks for the safety of their landing. The crumpled plane and the close call made the thought seem silly, as silly as it might look to a man like Mark McLaren.

No. I won't fall into feelings like that, thought Katie, and she resolutely set about praising God for their survival. She didn't know she was speaking out loud until she felt Laurie's head on her shoulder and heard the teenager's voice repeating her words.

The crunch of boots against rocks intruded. Mark was only a few feet away, watching with a strange mixture of interest and disgust. Katie's voice trailed off. "Heather's acting strangely."

"She's not the only one," he shot back, then knelt beside them. "Shock," he said at once. "Laurie, get me a blanket and bring that canteen, too."

Laurie stood up shakily and walked to the pile of camping gear Mark had taken off the plane. Katie's white suitcase looked strangely out of place, sitting in the middle of a grassy field. While Laurie retrieved the items he had asked for, Mark handed Katie her skirt, then took it back again. He wadded it up and slipped it under Heather's head as he lowered her to the ground. The child did not protest being handled by him, a turnabout from her behavior at the airstrip a few hours before.

Mark covered her with the blanket Laurie had brought and unstopped the canteen. Heather drank thirstily, then sank back onto the ground with that same blank stare. Mark took her pulse and grunted.

"Will she be all right?" asked Katie.

"It isn't too bad."

"How do you know?"

"I'm a paramedic."

"Oh." Katie felt a rush of relief. "Lucky for us."

Mark sighed and stared at the *Adrian*. "A lot of things

were lucky for us. I was starting to think we weren't going to find a place to land, and I really didn't want to try Plan B or C. This little strip of land turned up just in time."

"That's the grace of God, Mr. McLaren."

"Nonsense. This land's been here for a million years, Reed. It didn't just spring into being because we needed to land on it."

"Were we on course?"

"What?"

"All that wind we ran into . . . were we still on course when the engine quit?"

Mark dropped his eyes, suddenly uncomfortable. "Not exactly. I was trying to get us around a storm. We weren't committed to any one route, you know. It's all right to change course to avoid foul weather. Is that okay with you?" he finished defensively, as if daring her to challenge him.

"That's my point, Mr. McLaren."

"What is?"

"This land didn't spring into being because we needed to land here. The Lord brought us right to it."

Mark regarded her curiously. "You believe that?"

"I do."

"You're a weird little bird, you know that?"

His smile kept his words from becoming an insult. Katie saw no mockery on his face. A thin stream of blood was seeping from a gash over his left eye. Katie gestured toward it. "You're bleeding."

"So are you," he said, and reached out to touch a deep scrape on her cheek. Katie breathed in sharply. His dark hazel eyes gleamed in his tanned face, and for an instant Katie thought she could follow him forever. The silliness of the thought made her wince, and Mark withdrew his hand at once. "I've got something to put on that," he said. "Let me tend to you, then we've got to set up camp."

"Camp?" Katie gaped at him. "What do we need a camp for?"

"Do you want to spend the night sitting on your suitcase?"

"Spend the night? Here?" Katie gestured at the field and woods.

Mark chuckled. "Were you expecting the Air Force already? I've got news for you—they're not coming. Someone will, but not tonight."

"But you called on the radio!"

"It's getting close to sundown. No one's going to come looking for us in the dark. I'll get a fire going, then set up. Don't look so worried, Reed. I admit it's not Glory Mountain, but wait until you see the stars out here. It's a sight you'll never forget."

Katie swallowed. "But someone will come after us tomorrow, won't they?"

"Probably, or the next day. It depends on the weather. You were smart to pick a plane filled with camping gear. I can even give you a choice between regular coffee and decaffeinated."

"A fire would be nice," Katie said, rubbing her hands together. "I guess I am getting a little cold."

Mark looked pointedly at the beige silk slip she was wearing. "Really? I can't imagine why."

Nerves and relief swelled up in Katie and bubbled over into laughter. Laurie snickered beside them and Mark joined in, their voices blending as if they'd been laughing together all their lives. Mark reached over and squeezed them both on the shoulder, then trudged off to get the first-aid kit. Katie watched his easy stride and decided that even though Mark McLaren was unsaved, he was a good man to have around in a crisis.

CHAPTER 4

KATIE HAD ALWAYS THOUGHT camping meant roasting wild game on a spit over a fire made by rubbing sticks together. She was pleasantly surprised to find Mark had a different idea. He served a Mexican dinner: boiling-bag taco filling spooned into burritos and served with nachos, shredded provolone, and coffee. The cooking aromas and the crackling fire lent a festive, holiday atmosphere to their predicament, almost as if it had been part of the outing from the beginning.

Only Heather had shunned the food and company; after she refused both Laurie and Katie's coaxing and turned coldly away from Mark's, she fell asleep by the fire. Mark moved her into a down sleeping bag inside a small tent he had set up for the girls. The firelight flickered yellowly against it, blending its silhouette naturally into the contours of the landscape. The tent looked as if it had been there forever. Only the price sticker still stuck to the flap over the zippered doorway gave it away.

Katie savored her last burrito and sipped her coffee, which seemed to taste better made over an open fire. The cheerful warmth and autumn fragrance of the burning wood gave her a sense of safety and well-being, like being at a Girl Scout jamboree.

Laurie was quiet, as if remembering other campfires in other times in other places. Katie let her own mind wander. She was slightly disturbed by her own curiosity. Why did Mark McLaren's daughters recoil from him? Why had they been separated for the last year? And what had happened to Adrian McLaren?

Laurie got up from her seat near the fire and opened a pack her father had placed nearby. She pulled out a long pink blanket sleeper, frowned at it, then checked the size tag and groaned. "I was afraid of that," she said to Katie. "It's too big. I guess he thought I'd grow more."

Katie shrugged. "It's better than being too small."

Katie watched her move with the assurance that came from experience. Laurie unzipped the tent and pushed her sleeping bag inside, then extended her feet out the flap to remove her shoes without bringing dirt and ashes inside. Katie watched her with envy, wishing this experience of sleeping outside wasn't so foreign to her.

"Good night, Miss Reed," came Laurie's muffled voice. "Just unzip the flap and come on in when you're ready."

Katie suddenly realized she wasn't equipped to camp out. She had no sleeping bag, no bedding, and no sensible blanket sleeper like Laurie's. She had only packed for the comfort of Glory Mountain Lodge. Mark had only packed for his own family, and for the first time she felt like an intruder, a houseguest who had arrived uninvited and empty-handed. Even the food she had eaten was intended for someone else.

"I think I'll just stay out here by the fire," she said uncertainly, not even sure the small tent could hold three people.

"You'll freeze," said Laurie. "The temperature really drops at night in the mountains."

"I have a sweater in my suitcase."

"It won't be enough. Besides, you've got a wool blanket and a sleeping bag in here."

"What?"

"Dad said this is the girls' dormitory, and no one's going to freeze while he's in charge."

Katie was taken aback. "He gave me his sleeping bag? What's he going to use?" She looked over at the smaller tent, a backpacker's tent that was barely large enough for two.

"He's used to roughing it." Laurie reached outside for her pack and pulled out her hairbrush. "He's been camping in these mountains for years, and besides, you can't win any arguments with him and you'll wind up using his stuff anyway."

Katie looked around in the darkness beyond the perimeter of their camp, searching for Mark. He was nowhere in sight. He had taken off to the west right after he packed the rest of their food in a box that looked like a dog carrier and hoisted it up into a tree about thirty feet away. He had answered Katie's questioning look with one word, "animals," and now Katie began to wonder just what kind of animals he had in mind.

Katie stood up and brushed off her skirt, annoyed that it looked so rumpled. She struggled between her timidity and the temptation to go looking for him. She heard Laurie zip the tent shut and unzip her sleeping bag, and felt suddenly alone. Katie debated for a moment, then strolled to the western edge of the camp. She could see the outline of the *Adrian*'s rudder and empennage silhouetted in the distance, a lonely monument marking their unintended stay in this lonesome part of the Montana Rockies.

As Katie's eyes adjusted to peering through the dark, she picked out Mark's outline standing near the downed plane. He was standing still. On an impulse Katie walked toward him, grateful for his caretaking and oddly lonely for his company, although it had been offensive most of the time.

Something skittered across her path and disappeared into the brush. Katie stopped, her heart pounding. The air had turned chilly, and the wind had picked up since nightfall. It swooshed through the thick branches of the tall pines, perfuming the air with the scent of Christmas. The world had turned exotic, and Katie was surprised to find herself enjoying it.

She stood just behind Mark, suddenly feeling awkward and unsure of herself.

"Hi," she said, annoyed by her own whispery voice. "I just found out I have some more things to say thank you for."

Mark didn't turn around. "Then go take a hike and say it where I can't hear it. Your religion makes me sick."

Katie felt stabbed. "I meant to thank *you*, Mr. McLaren. It was very kind of you to give me your sleeping bag—"

"It's really wrecked, you know. The left wing is almost torn off and the landing gear is snapped off completely. It'll never be safe to fly again."

"I'm sorry about your airplane."

"I make my living with that plane."

"I'm sorry."

"My plane! It was all I had left." Mark's voice was husky and ragged. The shock had finally hit him.

Katie's disappointment vanished and she began to feel sorry for him. "I really wish there was something I could do."

"Pray it back together."

"What?"

"You can't, can you? You think you've got some kind of pull with the King of creation, but you can't do anything to fix that wreck."

"Maybe things will look better in the morning." It sounded inane even to Katie.

"Do you think my plane will look any better? It's going to be just the same tomorrow as it is now. A pile of junk plowed into the ground. You can't fix it, and your God can't fix it." Mark jerked around to face Katie. "And by the way, don't go filling Laurie's head with all that religious talk. She's at the age when she'll buy anything. Leave her alone."

The barb went by Katie. She was too aware of his need for comfort to be offended. "Please don't worry, Mr. McLaren," she said softly. "After they rescue us tomorrow, everything will work out all right."

"Tomorrow," he said, with a snort.

"What?"

"Nothing. Go to bed, Reed."

"What about tomorrow?" Katie persisted.

"Nothing."

"They *are* coming, aren't they?"

"If they don't, maybe you can get a legion of angels to pick you up."

Katie turned away and walked quickly back to camp. Every good feeling she had felt for Mark McLaren had been crushed again. He had a way of surprising her with unexpected thoughtfulness and rugged capability, then killing the admiration as it barely began to live.

He'll kill us like Mommy. Katie recalled Heather's cryptic words and felt herself turning colder. She ran the last few steps and paused before the fire to warm herself. She could see her breath coming in short puffs, partly from exertion and partly from—what? Nerves? Fear?

Katie knelt to unzip the tent flap and backed in the way she had seen Laurie do, dangling her feet outside until she eased off her shoes. She thought both girls were asleep and quietly closed the flap again. She remembered then that her suitcase was still outside, but so was Mark, and that was reason enough not to go out again. She loosened her clothing as much as she could and crawled into the sleeping bag.

"Did you find him?" Laurie whispered.

"He's looking at the plane," Katie whispered back.

"Is he mad?"

"I think he's just upset."

Laurie leaned forward. "Don't you have anything else to wear to bed?"

"Nothing as warm as yours."

"Take my socks. If your feet are warm, you'll feel better."

"Thanks." Katie smiled in the darkness and groped around until she found Laurie's socks. She slipped them on over her snagged hose and started to unzip Mark's sleeping bag.

Heather stirred beside Laurie. She seemed to settle down again, but suddenly began to twist and jerk. "I don't want it!" she whined. "Take it off me!"

Laurie sat up. "Take what off?"

Heather squirmed around and opened her sleeping bag. She thrust out the blue plaid blanket she had been wrapped in. "I don't want it!"

"But Heather," said Katie, "you'll be cold without it."

"I don't want it. It's got blood on it!"

Laurie fumbled in the dark and came up with a five-cell flashlight. She turned it on the blanket. There was no sign of blood.

"I think you were dreaming," said Katie, relieved that the blanket was clean. "I'll trade blankets with you."

"S'okay," mumbled Heather. By the time Katie had her tucked in, she was asleep again.

"That was a little strange," whispered Katie, after Laurie turned off the light. "What do you think she meant by that?"

Laurie nestled into her own bag. "She was just remembering something that happened a couple years ago. She used to have dreams about it all the time."

"What happened?"

"A lady had an accident with her car near our house. She got out of the wreck and came up on our porch before she collapsed. Mom and Dad put that blanket on her and took care of her until the ambulance came."

"Did Heather see her?"

"Yeah. She was real scared, especially when the lady's heart stopped."

"She died?"

"Dad did mouth-to-mouth and she was okay after that."

Katie felt uncomfortable. She was angry and disgusted with Mark McLaren, and yet here she was in his sleeping bag listening to a story about him saving a stranger's life.

"She was lucky she picked your house," Katie offered, needing to say something nice.

"That's what everybody said. Even Grandma liked him back then."

Katie heard Laurie yawn and resisted the urge to ask any more questions. She pulled the blue plaid blanket up

51

over her shoulders and closed her eyes. The little tent quivered in the wind. Then Katie realized the wind had died and the tent was still shaking.

Something was trying to claw through the front flap.

Katie watched the flap moving and spotted sharp, tiny claws protruding through the mesh. She remembered Mark's concern about animals, and for a moment she imagined bears and mountain lions hovering outside the tent, waiting to pounce and devour her.

Laurie's hoarse voice broke through her terrified fantasy. "What is it? Katie, what is it?"

Katie could see Laurie's wide eyes fixed on the flap. Heather sat up slowly and stared, but said nothing. She clutched her princess doll in her arms and twisted her face as if she were crying, but no tears fell. Katie reached over and grabbed the long, heavy flashlight and trained it on the flap. All movement stopped. She could see nothing beyond the screen, but she sensed the intruder was still out there. She crawled out of the sleeping bag and moved up to the zippered flap, snapping the light off.

"Be careful," whispered Laurie.

Katie peered out the mesh. She could make out the campfire burning low, about fifteen feet away. A gust of cool air brought the aroma of charred wood wafting through the tent. There was no sign or sound of an animal outside.

"I think the light scared it away," said Katie.

Claws tore into the screen inches from her face. Katie gasped and jerked backward, then swung the flashlight around and thumped it against the flap. It thudded against a bulky, squirming thing. Katie heard it hiss, then the animal pitched itself against the flap and began to claw in earnest. Katie grabbed the flashlight with both hands and whacked at the beast. It squawked and backed away.

"Did it go?" asked Laurie.

Katie nodded. "I think so."

The animal flung itself against the mesh. Heather screamed. Katie struck it again and again, frantic now in her need to protect the girls. She heard the beast hissing and growling and saw the mesh beginning to tear under its weight. Katie pounded harder, then heard shouting from outside. She heard the impact of a heavy rock hit the ground outside the tent. Another rock hit dully on the beast itself, and it loosened its claws from the screen at once. Katie heard the scratch of its claws as it raced off into the woods.

Katie dropped the light and realized how hard she was trembling. Laurie held her by the shoulders, pressing close, giving her both the comforting hug of an adult and the clinging grasp of a frightened child.

Mark's voice floated in through the mesh. "Which one of you did that?"

"It was Katie," said Laurie. "I mean, Miss Reed."

"Not bad, Reed. I didn't figure you'd be one to take on a wolverine. I'm really impressed."

Katie found her voice. "A wolverine? Are they dangerous?"

"They can be vicious if they feel like it. Who's got food in there?"

"Food?" Katie exchanged a look with Laurie. "No one."

"Look in Heather's pack."

Laurie opened it and fished around inside.

Heather glared at her with her arms folded across her chest. "That's mine."

"Did you find anything?" prodded Mark.

"Candy bars." Laurie counted them out.

"Hand them over." Mark unzipped the tent flap.

"They're mine! Grandma gave them to me!"

"You can have them back tomorrow. Don't ever take food into your tent again. Your next visitor could be a hungry bear."

Laurie handed the candy out to Mark. "That's all of it."

"Hand out the pack, too. It might be carrying the scent. I'll string it up with the food box until it airs out."

Laurie scooted the pack past Katie. Mark reached in for it and touched Katie's hand. He squeezed it gently. "Not bad, Reed," he repeated. "Good night, everybody. I'm glad you're feeling better, Heather."

53

Heather grunted and turned over in silence. Katie murmured, "Good night," and listened to the crunch of his boots as he left their tent and walked off. Laurie crept back to her sleeping bag without another word. Katie waited by the flap, not sure why she was hesitating, listening intently to hear Mark's movements. She heard his steps coming back toward the fire, then finally tracing their way to his tent. She listened to the sound of the flap opening, then closing again. The camp became silent.

Katie crawled inside her own sleeping bag and lay down. She felt her heart racing, and only after Heather and Laurie were asleep did she realize it wasn't the wolverine that had quickened her pulse, but Mark's approval.

Katie could imagine Mary Grace frowning and shaking her head over this. She tried to push Mark out of her mind but kept focusing on his boyish grin and his shining hazel eyes. "Thank God we'll be out of here tomorrow," she whispered aloud, knowing that if she had to stay here any longer, she might make a fool of herself over another wrong man.

CHAPTER 5

KATIE WOKE TO THE AROMA of warm maple syrup. She stretched contentedly in the warmth of her cozy sleeping bag and sniffed the fragrance of frying bacon in the cool morning air. Camping wasn't as bad as she had thought it would be.

Her skirt and blouse were rumpled and she had a run in her stocking. She hesitated to go outside looking so unkempt, but her suitcase with her casual slacks and sweaters was still outside. She pulled off Laurie's socks and laid them at the foot of her sleeping bag, then slipped on her leather pumps and climbed out of the tent, leaving the girls still sleeping.

The air was cold and she shivered in her thin clothing. The first thing she saw were the tracks around the flap. They were much bigger than she had expected, and her stomach turned at the thought of such a large animal trying to reach them last night.

Mark was kneeling by the fire, expertly flipping pancakes in a black iron skillet. "Here comes the big game hunter." He looked her up and down. "Are you all over being scared yet?"

Katie drew herself up sharply. She didn't want him to think she was a coward. "I'm fine."

"You'll be finer after you change into something more—"

"I know. Presentable."

"I was going to say practical."

"That's what I meant."

"I've got some water heated for you."

"What for?"

"To wash up with. You didn't plan to go swimming in the lake, did you?"

"Is there a lake around here?"

"No, just a stream. It's that way." Mark gestured with the spatula. "We sure were lucky to find a landing strip so close to fresh water."

Katie knew luck had nothing to do with it and almost said so, but she felt foolish enough standing in the chilly air shivering in her creased clothing.

Mark flipped a pancake. "Breakfast is almost ready, so you'd better hurry up."

Katie hesitated. "Is it safe?"

"To go to the stream? No way. I don't want anybody walking around out there alone. You can get lost two hundred feet from camp in woods like these. Just take the bucket and go behind your tent. I'm a gentleman. Besides, I'm busy."

Katie felt awkward. She picked up the bucket of warm water and picked her way over to the tent. Laurie crawled out and sniffed the air appreciatively, but Heather made a face.

"Yuck. I hate bacon," she complained.

"The bathroom's over here," said Katie. "Look. We've even got hot running water."

Laurie smiled thinly at the bucket. "He always did that for me when we went camping." Her smile vanished and was replaced by a frown.

"He never did it for me," said Heather petulantly.

"I never took you camping," said Mark from behind her. "Give me a break, okay?" He was carrying Katie's white suitcase. He set it down beside the bucket. "No tipping, ma'am. Bellhop service comes with this deluxe hotel."

"That's not funny," said Heather.

Mark gave her a long look.

Heather shrugged and turned her back on him. "I hate it here."

"Give it a chance," he said. "Breakfast is almost ready."

"It sure smells good," said Katie.

Mark didn't answer. Katie thought she saw his shoulders slump as he walked around the tent.

"Bacon and pancakes are fattening," Heather said.

"You're only six," said Laurie. "What do you care?"

"Grandma would say it was fattening."

Katie dressed in her forest green wool pants and pulled a soft turquoise sweater over her head. Heather watched her curiously. "Don't you have any jeans? I mean, you're kind of dressed up for camping."

"I didn't pack for camping," Katie said. "I was expecting to be at a very comfortable lodge today." She was already feeling silly that she had chosen her best casual outfit. "Besides," she added, "I want to look nice when the rescue planes come. Maybe they'll take pictures and we'll be in the newspaper."

"Are they coming today?" asked Heather hopefully. "I want to go back to Grandma's."

"Don't get your hopes up," said Laurie. "They have to find us first."

"Don't they know where we are?" asked Katie. "I heard your father on the radio giving directions."

"They still have to spot us."

"Will it take long?"

"I don't know. Ask Dad. He's the one who knows about airplanes." Katie thought she heard that same faint note of pride in Laurie's voice, hiding underneath the offhanded hostility.

But there was no pride in Heather's voice. Her dislike for her father was coldly paraded every time she spoke. Katie pulled on her wool socks and loafers, watching the little girl and wondering again what she had meant when she had cried in the plane, "He's going to kill us like Mommy."

"Come on, gang!" called Mark. "I can't hold out much longer!"

Mark had spread a colorful patchwork quilt out beside the fire, lending a picnic atmosphere to breakfast. He had filled three metal pans with pancakes, topped with butter that had already started to melt and run down the sides of the stacks in creamy yellow rivers. Bacon was tucked neatly around the sides. Katie felt another twinge of guilt for taking their food, and now their dishes, for Mark was eating off a square of aluminum foil with the edges curled up. The girls hung back, neither of them wanting to claim a place near their father. Katie wondered if he noticed.

If he did, he didn't show it. He gestured for Katie to sit down and she took the place closest to him. The girls sat down on the other side of her.

"There's more where that came from," he said, "so dig in."

Katie folded her hands and bowed her head automatically. Mark hesitated, a strip of bacon halfway to his mouth, then set it back on his makeshift plate. He sighed heavily, as if he were humoring a child. "Go ahead, Reed. Get it over with."

Katie felt a self-conscious flush warming her face. She closed her eyes. "Lord, we thank you for bringing us here safely and protecting us from the wolverine last night . . ."

"You did that," said Heather.

". . . and for providing this beautiful day and this breakfast."

"Dad made breakfast," said Laurie.

Katie's flush deepened. "Please help the rescue planes to find us quickly. . . ."

"Amen!" said Heather. "I want to go home."

Mark glanced at Katie. "Now?"

She nodded. He sighed again and began eating.

"When will the rescue planes get here?" asked Katie as she picked up her plate.

Mark shrugged. "No telling."

"But it's been over twelve hours since we crashed."

"We didn't crash." Mark slapped his fork down on his makeshift plate. "We landed."

58

"I'm sorry—but it's still been twelve hours."

"They're probably out looking for us already. Don't worry about it. Enjoy nature. I'll bet this is the first and last time you'll ever go camping, so make the most of it." Mark's voice had become brittle, and he kept his eyes on his plate.

Katie felt a strange feeling come over her, a sensation that he wasn't telling the whole truth. "But they will get here today, won't they?"

Mark twisted his lip impatiently. "How should I know? I'm not in charge of air rescues in Montana. They'll get here when they get here. Get off my back."

"Don't talk to her like that!" snapped Laurie. "It's not her fault we're stuck here!"

"It's your fault!" added Heather, staring at her father. "We didn't want to come here, anyway."

"Tell me something I don't already know," said Mark angrily. He got up abruptly and walked away from the fire.

"It's his fault," Heather repeated. "He didn't even ask Grandma if we could come. He just came and got us. Grandma said she was going to call the police if he made us get on the airplane, but he didn't listen. He pulled me." She displayed an arm that didn't have a mark on it. "See, he hurt me."

Katie shifted uncomfortably. "It doesn't look like he hurt you very much."

"He hurt me, all right."

"Don't defend him," said Laurie, turning on Katie. "He's been treating you like dirt, too."

"No, he hasn't. How can you say that? Look at this breakfast. Look how he made it look like a picnic. He's been doing all the work setting up the camp and taking care of us, and all the time he's been upset about the damage to his airplane. You don't have any reason to criticize him." Katie felt her voice rising in pitch and she broke off.

Heather stuck out her lip and turned her back to Katie.

Laurie ate in silence for a few moments, then said, "It's all a trick to get us back."

59

"Why do you think he wants you back?"

Laurie looked up sharply. "What?"

"Did you ever stop to think that if he's trying to get you back he must love you very much?"

Laurie blinked back tears. "I don't care if he loves us. It's too late now."

"We don't love him," said Heather. "We'll never love him again."

Katie struggled with her desire to know more and the feeling that it was none of her business. She studied Heather, so small and delicate, hunched over and pouting. Katie wanted to say something that would make her feel better, more inclined to see some good in her father, but she didn't know how to approach the child. She had never seen such hostility in one so small.

A twig snapped behind Katie. She jerked around, half-expecting to see the wolverine. At first she saw nothing, then began to make out the sheen of fur nestled among the leaves. Two shining eyes peered back at her.

"Look!" she said softly. "It's a raccoon!"

Heather twisted around quickly, her anger vanishing. She squealed in excitement and jumped to her feet. "A raccoon! Oh, it's a baby!"

"Heather! Don't!" shouted Mark. He bounded over to her and seized her around the waist. She kicked at him, knocking the last of his breakfast out of his hand onto the quilt.

"Let me go!" she shouted. The raccoon chattered and scurried away into the woods.

"Put her down," growled Laurie. "She didn't do anything."

"Yes she did, and you know it. What's the first thing I ever taught you about wild animals?"

Laurie shrugged and looked down, not wanting to cooperate.

"You leave them alone," Mark continued. "This is real life, not some kiddie movie on TV. These animals aren't tame and harmless. They'll bite and claw you if you come too close to them. Don't ever walk up to a wild animal, no matter how cute it looks, and especially not baby animals. Their mothers might be nearby."

"I wish mine was," said Laurie.

Heather fought out of her father's grip. "I wish mine was!" she repeated, then sobbed raggedly and ran back toward the tent. She fumbled with the zipper and crawled inside.

Mark whirled on his older daughter. "Oh good, Laurie! What did you have to say that for?"

"It's true."

Mark shook his head and walked over to his gear. He picked up an ax and turned to look back. "Keep an eye on them, Reed. Don't let them wander away from the camp."

"I never wander away!" shouted Laurie. "I know how to camp!"

"You didn't remember to keep away from wild animals."

"I did so! That was Heather, not me!"

"You should've stopped her."

"I would have if you hadn't butted in!"

Mark stalked off among the trees.

Katie touched Laurie's shoulder. "Calm down, please. We shouldn't be fighting."

"He started it!"

"It doesn't matter who started it. We can't tear at each other like this. It won't help at all."

"Nothing can help," said Laurie. "Everything's rotten and it's all his fault."

"Why? What did he do that made you so angry with him?"

"He left us! Right after Mom died—" Laurie stood up quickly. "I don't want to talk about it." She dropped her empty plate on the quilt and half-ran to the tent where Heather had taken refuge.

Katie began to gather up the dishes, then stopped. She placed her head in her hands and felt tension flood through her body. The churning inside grew faster and more powerful until she was overwhelmed with the burden to pray for these two angry children and the father they despised. She prayed aloud, rushing and stumbling over the words that poured forth from her heart and spilled over her lips.

At last she stopped, feeling spent and tired, yet contented that something good had finally taken place. In the distance she could hear the ax thumping against a tree trunk, and she lifted her face to the piercing blue sky and breathed in the fragrance of flowers and the pine-scented air. This time when she reached out for the peace beyond understanding, it was there.

CHAPTER 6

KATIE GATHERED UP THE DISHES from the quilt, trying to make herself a useful guest, but found herself distracted by the stark mountains that surrounded her. Above the bluish sheen of the fir trees the rock turned gray and barren, lancing the sky like giant spearheads. She could see the silvery-white snowcaps on the peaks, and she shivered involuntarily at the thought of how cold it must be at the tops of those rugged cliffs. The morning air was thick with dew, permeating the camp with an after-storm fragrance of wet soil.

She pulled at her sweater, as if she could somehow make it warmer, and wished she had brought her ski jacket from home. Her dressy wardrobe made her feel even more out of place and incapable in this remote wilderness where Mark McLaren was so much at home. She felt a twinge of envy when Laurie finally emerged from the tent, properly dressed in heavy denim jeans and a cable-knit sweater topped by a red down vest. She, like her father, belonged here, just as Katie did not.

The envy faded when Katie saw Laurie's face. The evidence of crying was still fresh on her pale cheeks, her eyes red-rimmed and irritated from rubbing. Katie wondered how much of the crying had been caused by the stress of the emergency landing, and how much of it came from memories of her mother's death.

Laurie took the dishes from Katie's hands, avoiding her eyes. "Here, I'll do that. There's a special way you have to wash dishes out here."

Katie felt incompetent, again. "How?"

"You have to wash them in a dishpan or a bucket, so you won't get soap into the natural waters and hurt the fish and animals. When you're done, you dump the water into a trench with cut boughs over it, to absorb the food smells and the soap. Later on we'll put the boughs on the fire and clean up once and for all." Although her face was still pinched and strained, Laurie seemed to enjoy teaching Katie.

"It sounds like you've got a lot of respect for nature."

"It's too beautiful out here to mess it up with detergents and trash," said Laurie. "I know where Dad keeps the trowel, so I'll go dig the trench while you get started on these."

"He didn't want you to leave the camp."

"I won't go far enough to matter. Besides, I've got this." She pointed to a large silver whistle on a chain around her neck. "If you hear three blasts, you'll know I'm lost or in trouble."

"That's a good idea. Does Heather have one, too?"

"She said she wouldn't wear it. She thinks it's a present from Dad, not just standard camping gear. She doesn't want anything from him that looks like a present. I don't think we'll ever get her into her blanket sleeper. He bought it, you know."

"I guess she's angry with him, too. Just like you are." Katie smiled gently. "You both must have been very hurt."

Laurie looked away quickly. "He just shouldn't have left us, that's all." She hesitated, as if she wanted to say more, then strode off toward Mark's gear beside his tent.

Katie watched for Heather while she washed the dishes, but the child refused to come out of the tent. Laurie carried the water bucket away to dump it and came back with an armful of sticks for the fire. She showed familiarity with the wilds with every step she took. As she knelt to feed the fire Katie caught for the first time a faint resemblance between her and her father.

Katie peered up at the sky and was startled by its vivid blueness.

"Looking for planes?" asked Laurie. "I guess you really want to get out of here, too."

"Oh, I don't know," said Katie. "It's beautiful out here. I've never been out of the city in my life."

Laurie shot her a look of shocked sympathy. "Never? How did you stand it? I'd like to build a cabin and live out here in the wilderness. I hate living in the city."

"Have you camped out often?"

Laurie nodded. "We used to do it every weekend in the summer when Dad wasn't on duty."

"On duty?"

"At the fire station. He rode ambulance duty."

"That's right, he's a paramedic."

"And when he had to work too many weekends in a row, he'd sometimes take off in the middle of the week. Once he even took me out of school to go with him."

"Is that where you learned so much about camping?"

"Doing it is the best way to learn it."

"Too bad we're being rescued today. This is probably the only chance I'll ever get," said Katie, surprised by her own regret.

"It might not be today, but I hope it is."

"I thought you said you liked it out here."

"I do, but—"

Katie knew what she meant. The friction between Mark and his daughters was starting to wear on them all. Laurie got busy tending the fire unnecessarily, her gestures and mannerisms almost a duplicate of her father's. Katie watched her and thought, *it wouldn't take much for her to love him again.*

Mark came back into camp, carrying a long-handled ax in his hand. He gestured toward the girls' tent. "Is Heather still in there?"

"Yes," said Katie.

"Go get her, Laurie. I want to show you girls how to get around without getting lost."

65

Laurie obediently went to the tent. While she was gone, Katie studied Mark. He blended into the landscape as perfectly as Laurie did, dressed properly in a wool sweater and blue down vest. Katie saw the sheath of a knife protruding from under the vest and thought how appropriate it seemed for him.

He began to clean off the handle of the ax. "Porcupines'll ruin an ax handle trying to lick off the salt," he said. "I've got to remember to take my gloves next time."

"Are there porcupines around here?"

"We've got just about everything around here. I saw a bobcat down by the stream, and there are deer tracks all over the place. I saw a couple of jack rabbits, too, and every squirrel in a ten-mile radius came to look me over while I was working."

"You must have cut lots of firewood. You were gone for an hour."

Mark shook his head. "I was blazing trees. When I take you over there you'll see the marks I made so you can find your way down to the stream and back without getting lost." He looked her up and down and grinned. "In case I didn't say it, you look nice."

Katie felt herself blushing. "It's not very rugged. Glory Mountain Lodge is a far cry from this place."

Mark lost his smile. "Not far enough."

Laurie came back, dragging a scowling Heather behind her. Heather dug in her heels and fought her sister all the way. "I don't want to go anywhere with him!"

"Where's your whistle?" demanded Mark. "Didn't Laurie tell you to keep it on?"

Laurie held up a silver whistle. "Of course I told her. She won't wear it. That's not my fault."

"Wear it!" said Mark firmly. "If you get lost, it's the only way we have to find you again." He snatched it from Laurie's hand and draped it over Heather's head. She reached up at once to remove it, but he locked his hand over her wrist. "Leave it!"

Heather's defiant look crumpled and she dropped her hand.

Mark took them to the trees he had notched and showed them how to follow the line back and forth to the narrow, bubbling stream. "I'll get back out here tomorrow and cut more," he said, "so eventually we'll have trail guides from the camp like spokes on a wheel. I don't want anyone out exploring alone, but if you take a wrong turn it shouldn't be too hard to find your way back. If you can't, use your whistles." He glanced at Katie, then pulled his own silver whistle from around his neck and handed it to her. "Three blasts is the universal signal for help."

"Laurie told me," said Katie, and saw a faint smile touch the girl's lips.

Mark nodded appreciatively. "She's always been quite a trooper."

"But what will you do if you get lost?" asked Katie. "I've got your whistle."

"I'll stand where I am and holler like crazy until you come to find me."

"I won't come," muttered Heather.

"Go on," urged Mark, "try to follow the markers back to the camp."

Laurie and Heather turned away at once and began the trek back to camp, but Katie lingered behind. "Mr. McLaren, I'm sure you know what you're doing, but—"

"But what, Reed?"

"Aren't these kind of elaborate things to do for a camp we'll be leaving? I mean, shouldn't you be building a signal fire or something instead?"

Mark became uncomfortable. "I'll get to that next."

"Why not first? I mean, why not make us all stay together so we won't get lost, instead of blazing trails?"

"I know what I'm doing!"

"I'm sure you do, but—"

"Survival always takes precedence, Reed. It won't do any good for the rescue planes to show up if we're scattered so far apart they can't round us all up."

"Is there some other reason for all this?"

"Such as?"

Katie swallowed. "You don't think they're going to find us?"

"They'll be looking."

"But you're acting like we're going to be here for a long time."

"The first plane that sees us isn't going to stop and pick us up. They'll report our location, and we'll be picked up later, probably by helicopter. This isn't the greatest terrain for landing small planes, in case you hadn't noticed."

"But shouldn't we have a signal fire going by now?"

"We don't need one yet. If we hear a plane, we'll switch on the ELT. That's enough to guide it to our general area. The signal fire's just to help the second plane, or chopper, zero in on us visually."

"What's an ELT?"

"It's an Emergency Location Transmitter. I never fly without one. It beats the heck out of smoke signals when you're serious about being seen."

Katie felt a rush of relief. "I thought we didn't have a radio."

"The *Adrian*'s radios are dead. The ELT's just fine." Mark stuck his hands in the pockets of his vest. "I'm sorry you got stuck out here like this. I guess I owe you one."

Katie smiled and started to reassure him, but something large and black suddenly rose up behind him. She saw it over his shoulder and gasped aloud. Mark whirled around.

Bear.

Katie froze, unbelieving. It was less than twenty feet away, a mass of black fur with an immense round head and a brown muzzle jutting out below gleaming black eyes. It bawled ominously, its jaws opening to reveal its long, curved teeth.

"Get ready to run," Mark hissed.

Katie's body was leaden with terror. "Run? Where?"

"Anywhere but camp. Don't lead it to the girls." Mark stepped backward to interpose his body between Katie and the bear. "If he charges, don't wait for me to tell you. Just run."

Katie could smell it now, an awful odor of fish, oil, and

musk. It swayed on its hind legs, its front paws moving side to side, long claws sweeping the air. Mark swallowed noisily, then spread out his arms. He made a "whuff" sound, then advanced a step. The bear stared at him. He waved his arms again. "Whuff!"

The bear lowered its front legs to the ground. It regarded him uncertainly, then turned and lumbered off into the forest. Mark sagged with relief, then turned back to Katie and grabbed her by the arm. He propelled her in front of him until she recovered her senses and began to run. They jogged back toward the camp, Mark twisting around to look back while Katie struggled to keep her balance on the rough ground.

They burst into the camp so abruptly both girls jumped to their feet. Mark immediately bolted for his tent, reached inside and pulled out a long, smooth rifle. He ran back to the edge of the campsite, scanning the trees and brush for any sign that they might have been followed. Katie's heart thumped so hard her head hurt. She seized a long piece of firewood and held it like a club in front of the girls.

"What is it?" asked Laurie.

"Bear," said Katie.

Heather whimpered and started toward the tent, but Laurie grabbed her by the hood of her red sweatshirt.

"No! You'll be trapped in there!" she warned.

Heather wheeled, and in panic wrapped her arms around Katie's waist. They waited tensely, watching the woods.

Mark finally lowered the rifle. "It didn't follow us."

"Thank God," breathed Katie.

Mark approached the fire cautiously, his eyes on his frightened daughter. "It's okay, Heather," he said. "It's gone."

"Your dad scared it off," said Katie. "He stood right up to it and roared at it and it ran away."

"Really?" asked Laurie. She watched Mark with eyes that shone with old admiration for a moment before she pulled her face back into its mask of cold indifference.

Mark knelt beside Heather. "It's okay now, sweetheart," he repeated, but Heather pressed closer to Katie.

69

"Why'd you make us come here?" she moaned, her voice muffled by Katie's sweater.

Mark stood up slowly. "Yeah," he said in a low voice. "Why?"

Heather clung to Katie for several minutes, then gradually let go and turned her attention back to the doll she was holding. Laurie moved beside her. Katie gave Heather's hair an affectionate stroke, then followed Mark to the edge of the camp, where he stood with his back to them and his rifle pointed muzzle down.

"Are you all right?"

"Sure," he said, a little too easily.

"I never saw anyone do that to a bear."

"You never saw a bear before, either." He glanced at the stick she still held in her hand. "What were you going to do? Beat it to death?"

"I thought it would make a nice rug for my living room floor."

"It would look great next to the wolverine pillows." Mark lifted the rifle, checked the action, then lowered it again. "I think I was saying something about being sorry I got you into this."

"You didn't. If I hadn't wanted to go to Glory Mountain, you'd be safe in a public campground right now."

"No, we wouldn't. I was trying to find a place just like this one, far away from other people. I wanted my girls to have to depend on me for everything."

"Why?"

"I wanted them to need me . . . or something like that. I mean, I shouldn't have been surprised that they didn't come running out to me yelling "Daddy" when I finally came home. It's been an entire year. I thought if I could just get them away from Adrian's mother for a while, let them get to know me again and see that I was still their father—" He broke off abruptly. "I'm sorry you got caught in the middle. You'll get a refund, of course."

"I don't care about that."

"It wasn't cheap."

"It wasn't my money. This trip was a wedding gift from a friend."

Mark looked at her sharply. "You're married?"

Katie flushed scarlet. "Well, no . . ."

Mark groaned. "Oh, no! You were going to get married up at Glory Mountain, weren't you?"

"No, no. I'm not getting married at all. We decided not to. I decided not to . . . I decided—"

"Decided what?"

"I couldn't marry a man who didn't love the Lord." Katie felt her face growing hot. The look on Mark's face told her how foolish her words sounded.

"You dumped the poor guy because of *that?*"

Katie was startled by the anger in his voice. His hazel eyes blazed through hers. His lips twisted into a sneer. "Well, if that's what you're like, I'd say he was lucky he got out in time. There's nothing worse than a Bible-thumping Jesus freak to drive you to—"

The underbrush rustled loudly. Mark's head snapped around. He thrust his arm out and scooped Katie behind him, then raised the rifle, ready to fire. A porcupine waddled into the clearing, raised its nose to sniff the air, and moved past them toward the stream.

"I thought that was the bear," whispered Mark.

"So did I," said Katie. She stood behind him awkwardly, not knowing what to do or say to break the heavy tension that arched between them. Mark didn't speak to her again, only stood with his back to her and his daughters and stared in the direction of the broken and disabled *Adrian.*

Katie left him there, wishing the rescue planes would come and at the same time wishing they would not. She was anxious to leave the dangers of the wilderness behind her, but the more she recoiled from Mark McLaren, the more she felt drawn to his mysterious past and his troubled present.

His attitude toward Christians was too hostile to reflect mere prejudice. There was more to it than that.

Katie dropped the stick on the pile of firewood and folded her arms, bracing herself against the cool breeze.

71

She wondered why Mark had left his children for a year.
She wondered why Heather held him personally responsible for her mother's death. Now she had a new
question: who was the Christian in Mark's past whom he
hated so much?

CHAPTER 7

AFTER LUNCH MARK PUT EVERYONE to work building the signal fire. Laurie announced that she was only helping because she was bored and needed something to do. Heather helped because she wanted to get back home as quickly as possible. The afternoon sunshine glowed against their shiny blond hair as they worked together.

Katie felt a stab of envy as she watched them carrying the wood their father cut and stacking it Lincoln-log style to form the base of the signal flame. Katie's chestnut hair and tall, robust build had never attracted boys the way the petite blond girls could, and she found herself imagining that Adrian McLaren had been one of those slim-hipped vixens she had always lost out to. The tall, athletic boys that had passed her by for the delicate flaxen-haired girls were the kind who grew up to look like Mark McLaren.

Katie reined in her jealous thoughts impatiently and turned her attention back to the job at hand. She picked up an armful of wood and moved gingerly down the hill, careful not to slip in her impractical loafers. The wood snagged her sweater, and she wished again she had Laurie's wardrobe instead of her own:

All around her was the evidence of nature unleashed.

Trees had been split and toppled, their bare tops telling of lightning damage. The clouds above her head had turned an ominous shade of gray in the last hour, and the wind had begun to gust in short blasts, sweeping leaves, twigs, and fine dust along with it. She scanned the sky anxiously. Would rescue planes turn around and go back if a storm began? How would they light a fire if the wood became rain drenched?

Mark seemed to read her mind. "I've got a tarp in the plane," he said conversationally, although it was the first time he had spoken to her in hours. "As soon as we're done here, I'll go get it and stretch it over the wood pile. From the look of those clouds, we're not going to get away with just a light shower."

Katie thought of her flimsy-looking tent and shivered. "I wish there were a good motel nearby."

"You might like it. There's nothing cozier than drifting off to sleep in a sleeping bag with rain tapping on the tent."

"It sounds like you expect us to be here all night again."

"We probably will. The sight of those clouds will keep light planes out of the area."

Katie felt an odd mixture of disappointment and relief. "Will the storm be over by tomorrow?"

"Hard to say. We may be in for a couple days of rain."

"Days?" Katie couldn't imagine huddling in a tent for more than one night in the rain. "Won't the rescue people be worried about leaving us stuck out here that long?"

"They'll search for us as long and as thoroughly as they can, but they won't take reckless chances and risk their planes and their lives. Don't worry, Reed. They'll get here eventually. Meanwhile, you've got that retreat you wanted, although with no preaching." Mark expertly whacked at a small tree with his long-handled ax. He handled the tool with the grace of long experience.

Katie watched him appreciatively. She had never been with a man who embodied such physical skill and confident capability. Most of the men she had dated were friends from her college Christian fellowship, those who had been attracted by her English major and her quiet but strong faith. She had gone to many fellowship outings and had taken part in more picnics, hayrides, and nature hikes than she could count now, but Mark's kind of rugged masculinity was new to her. She tried to imagine Steve bluffing a bear, and almost giggled at how ludicrous the thought was.

Mark retrieved the tarp from the *Adrian* and covered the ready-laid fire with it, careful to pull it down over the sides of the pyre to keep wind-carried rain from soaking through. Laurie automatically took hold of the tarp to help, and Katie sensed the unity with which they had once worked together. Mark tossed Laurie a line and she began to tie down the edge of the tarp, expertly knotting the rope with practiced fingers. Like her father, she slid a stick into the knot.

"What's that for?" asked Katie.

"To keep the rope from drying so tightly we can't get the knot untied," answered Laurie.

"You remember well," Mark said. "You always were handy to have around a campsite."

Laurie glowed momentarily, then froze over and ducked her head.

Her resentment is a powerful master, thought Katie. She felt her arms beginning to ache from the effort of lugging armfuls of wood, and she felt strangely tired for the middle of the day. She sat next to Heather, who had stopped working when the pyre reached up above her head, too high for her to help any longer. She was still cuddling her doll, and for the first time Katie got a close enough look at it to see that it resembled Heather. The doll watched them with its lifeless blue eyes, framed by hair as blond and shimmery as her owner's. She was dressed in blue silk and wore a homemade crown pinned in her hair. Katie wondered whether their grandmother had made it.

"What's your doll's name?"

"It's Aurora." Heather answered so quickly Katie realized how lonely and left out she was feeling. Her smile flashed in her delicate face. "It means dawn."

"That sounds familiar," said Katie, unable to place the name. "Who is she?"

"She's a princess," said Heather. "See her crown? Mommy made it. She made the dress, too. She made it look like the one in my storybook."

"She's very pretty."

"Princesses are always pretty. It's so princes will love them and save them."

"From dragons?" Katie tried to remember the plot of the story, but she wasn't sure which fairy tale Heather meant.

"From witches," said Heather. "Witches put spells on them and make them sleep a long time."

"That's right, I remember," said Katie. "Sleeping Beauty."

"She stuck her finger on a spindle. That's a spinning wheel. I have a picture of one in my book. They used to make yarn on them. That's how she fell asleep, when she stuck her finger on it."

"Didn't the prince have to fight a dragon anyway?"

"First he had to get through the giant thorns the witch put all around the palace." Heather's pretty face was comically intense as she related the story. "He had to use the sword of truth to cut them and get to her."

"Then he fought a dragon?"

"It was really the witch. She turned herself into a dragon to keep him from getting to Aurora and waking her up, but it didn't work. He killed that mean old witch." Heather mimicked a sword thrust.

"Then what happened?" asked Katie, enjoying Heather's enthusiasm.

"Then he went into the palace and up the stairs and found her."

Katie nodded. "And then?"

Heather's animated face suddenly deadened. The light went out of her eyes. She cuddled the doll close to her. "He broke the evil spell and made her wake up and be alive again."

Katie noticed her abrupt change of mood. She instinctively nudged closer and slipped her arm around the little girl's shoulders. "And they lived happily ever after, right?"

Heather didn't answer right away. She watched her father and sister tie down the tarp.

"Right?" urged Katie.

"That was because her prince came. It doesn't work if the prince doesn't come. You just stay dead if the prince doesn't come home." Heather's lips trembled.

Katie rushed to comfort her. "But he did come, Heather. He broke the spell and made everything all right again."

Heather raised solemn eyes to Katie's.

"No," she said. "He didn't come home at all."

Thunder crashed directly above them. Heather cried out and dropped the doll in the dirt at her feet. She stared at it for a moment and saw a fat raindrop strike the creamy white face. Katie reached out and picked it up for her.

"We just made it!" shouted Mark. "Let's get back to camp!"

Heather didn't move. Katie pulled her up to her feet. Raindrops plunked on her hair, and she pulled the hood of Heather's sweatshirt up over her head. "Let's go, honey," she urged. "We'll get wet if we stay here."

Heather reached up and took Katie's hand.

By the time they got back to the tent, rain had begun to pelt them viciously. The impact spat white ash upward from the burned-out campfire, and the cold logs crumbled into powder. Laurie was the last to crawl into the tent, her hair plastered against her cheeks. "That takes care of our rescue for today."

"It's still early," said Katie. "Can't they still come after the storm's over?"

"This kind of storm won't be over today."

"I want to go home now!" Heather sulked.

"Maybe tomorrow," said Katie.

Laurie took out her hairbrush and began to work at her tangled hair. "You better change clothes," she told Katie. "It gets cold when the rain starts, and you're wet."

Katie remembered her white suitcase, inconveniently placed outside the tent. She considered crawling out to get it, but another clap of thunder made her think twice. The rain began to fall harder. Borne by the wind, it struck hard against the side of the tent as well as the top.

"Room service," said Mark from outside. A moment later he pushed her suitcase through. Katie pulled it out of the way just as he tossed in a foil bag. "Take a handful and give me the bag back," he said. "I still don't like having food in the tents."

They were gingersnaps. Katie sniffed their fragrant, pungent scent and realized she was ravenous. She distributed the cookies among the three of them and handed back the bag.

"Don't keep them," he warned. "Eat them and get it over with."

"Thank you," said Katie, annoyed that neither of the girls had expressed any gratitude. Mark left the tent and she closed the flap.

Laurie brushed her wet hair sullenly, occasionally taking a vicious bite of cookie, but Heather left hers on the sleeping bag beside her. She was rocking the doll in her arms, and she bent over and kissed it on the lips. Instantly she lifted the doll up, as if it had sprung to life and began to dance it around.

Katie watched intently, suddenly aware that there was something significant in Heather's fantasy game.

"Heather," she said, "when you were telling me the story of Sleeping Beauty, you said the prince didn't come home. What did you mean?"

Heather shrugged. Laurie looked up with a frown. "That's not right. The prince came. That's how the story ended."

"Uh-huh," agreed Heather. She laid down on the sleeping bag and stuck a gingersnap in her mouth.

Katie felt uneasy, as if something had started and hadn't been finished. She didn't know what to do or say, and Heather seemed content to turn her back and ignore them. Katie reached under her blanket and pulled out her Bible. The pages were velvety smooth from long use, and she turned quickly to the story of the disciples in the boat during the storm of the Sea of Galilee.

"What are you reading?" asked Laurie. When Katie told her, she nodded. "I remember that one from Sunday school."

"I didn't know you went to Sunday school."

"We haven't since . . ." Laurie stole a cautious look at Heather. ". . . since Mom died. You can read out loud if you want. I'm bored anyway."

Katie read the story, unsure whether anyone was really listening to her. When she finished, Laurie offered no comments but Heather rolled over. "Did Jesus really make the storm stop?"

"Yes, he did."

Heather rolled her eyes upward, where rain thudded against the canvas over their heads. "Wow."

"I wish he was here to calm this one," said Laurie. "I don't like to sleep in the rain. I'm always afraid the tent's going to fill up with water."

"Could it?" asked Katie nervously.

"Could it?" Heather repeated, her eyes bulging.

"No, it just sounds like it could. Read some more, Miss Reed."

Heather giggled. "Read, Reed."

She sounded just like Mark when she spoke Katie's name. Katie began to turn pages, searching for an appropriate story, and paused to listen to the staccato thumping of the rain. Thunder rumbled, until Katie realized that it wasn't thunder anymore but a low-pitched bawling noise, coming from outside their tent.

Katie froze. She had heard that sound before.

Laurie wasn't aware of it. "You ought to read us the one about Noah's ark," she said. "It sounds like it might rain for forty days."

Katie leaned close to the mesh and forced herself to look out.

The bear was in the camp. It prowled around underneath the food box, strung thirty feet over its head. The bear raised up on its back legs and pawed the air, as if it couldn't understand why it smelled food. Katie watched, paralyzed, as it backed down on all fours, walked around in a slow circle, then reared up again.

"What's the matter?" asked Laurie. "Is a flood coming?"

"No," said Katie. "Don't make any noise."

Laurie dropped her brush. "Why not? What's out there?"

"Ssshh."

Laurie inched forward and looked out the flap. "Oh, no!"

"What is it?" demanded Heather in a squeaky voice.

"Nothing."

"Yes, it is something! What is it?"

"Be quiet! It's just an animal!"

"What kind of animal?"

"A big one, that's all. Don't worry." But Heather was sitting up now, clutching her doll.

The bear sniffed the air, frustrated by the pouring rain and the scent of unseen food.

"The cookies!" whispered Katie suddenly. "Are there still cookies in here?"

There were two. Heather grabbed them and stuffed them both in her mouth. Outside, the bear turned around again, then sniffed in the direction of the girls' tent.

"Oh, no," moaned Laurie in a whisper. "Did he smell them?"

"I don't know." Katie saw the bear had turned away again, but didn't seem to know which direction to go in. It stood and swayed, its brownish-tan snout poised in the air.

Laurie reached for the flashlight and passed it to Katie. She stared at it and almost laughed. It was ridiculously small to use against something as huge and powerful as a black bear. Katie felt an urge to scream for Mark, but knew the sound might attract the bear. She tightened her grip on the flashlight.

The bear was facing their tent again. It bawled a complaint.

"Is it coming after us?" asked Heather. "Don't let it get us, Katie! Please!"

80

"It's not coming in here!" snapped Laurie.

The bear began to lumber toward them.

"Jesus, help us," whispered Katie. Laurie glanced at her, eyes wide in alarm. Heather was whimpering.

"Amen!" her little voice quavered.

The bear came closer. Katie gripped the flashlight and felt it slip in her sweating hands.

"Katie!" cried Laurie.

The bear stopped and pricked up its ears. Laurie covered her mouth with her hands.

"Jesus, help us," Katie repeated.

The bear took another step. A sharp crack cut above the noise of the rain and the bear jumped backward. It bawled again, and a second shot cracked the din and impacted somewhere on the ground in front of the bear.

The bear reared up, turning its head around wildly, looking for the danger. It dropped to all four feet and fled from the camp, leaving large muddy tracks on the wet ground.

Heather grabbed Katie from behind and pressed against her. Katie reached back to touch the terrified child. "It's all right," she soothed. "Your father made it go away. It's gone."

She sensed rather than heard his approach. "Are you all right in there?"

"We're fine," said Katie. "Just a little scared."

"Heather? Laurie?"

"They're all right, Mark."

Laurie heaved a sigh. "You missed it."

"I meant to. The last thing I wanted was a wounded bear ten feet from your tent."

"Thank you," said Katie, both to Mark and to God. "You came just in time."

"It's about time I did something right." His voice came through the flap. "I wish I could take credit, but it was just a coincidence I happened to look outside when I did."

Katie smiled thinly. Sure it was.

"Listen, Reed," he went on, "the rain's starting to slacken down. I'm going to try to get a fire going as soon

81

as it stops. You could all probably use a hot drink. How does hot chocolate sound?''

"I want to go home!" said Heather. "Isn't the plane going to come and get us?"

Mark hesitated. "Maybe," he said at last, "but don't count on it."

The rescue plane didn't come that night. Katie lay in Mark's sleeping bag, unable to sleep for fear of the bear's return, and she cradled her Bible in her arm like a teddy bear. Her soft blue nightgown was more decorative than warm, and she was grateful for the loan of the down bag, knowing how uncomfortable she would have been without it. She felt another twinge of guilt, knowing Mark was making do with two heavy wool blankets folded and pinned together. He could be hostile and obnoxious at times, but underneath he was really a prince.

A prince.

Katie frowned, remembering Heather's recital of the fairy tale. Something clicked in her memory. She tried to focus her attention on a thought that kept slipping away. She knew she had been given a clue to Heather's mysterious comment about Mark "killing us like Mommy," but she didn't know what it meant.

A low roar rumbled above her. She tensed hopefully. A plane? The roar persisted, then became louder. Lightning flashed brightly, illuminating the interior of the tent. It was not a plane. Only thunder. Rain began to beat against the tent again.

Katie rolled over and felt the heavy five-cell flashlight pressing on her arm. She reached for it, then pulled it under the sleeping bag and snapped it on. The brilliance of the light hurt her eyes for a moment, but she focused the beam on her Bible and opened it.

"There is a time for everything, and a season for every activity under heaven . . . ," she read. She clicked off the light and listened to the rain. "What is the reason, Lord? Why am I out here? Did you send me, or was it just an accident?"

"Katie," said Heather.

"What is it, honey?" answered Katie, but she saw that the girl was only talking in her sleep.

"Katie," said Heather again, then she nestled into her bag and fell silent.

Katie listened to the storm raging outside and knew there was a more violent storm inside of Heather, and Laurie, and Mark himself. The thought of Mark nearby, probably sitting up with his rifle in his hand, watching over their sleep, made her feel warm inside and tingly in a way she had never before experienced.

"I won't believe it's an accident," she whispered in the dark. "I believe there's a purpose, and whatever it is, please let me help them all, just a little bit."

CHAPTER 8

MARK SHOVELED OATMEAL INTO TIN BOWLS and passed them around along with a plastic bag filled with brown sugar. The hot cereal smelled so wonderful that Katie felt a little faint, the result of missing dinner the evening before. She dug in gratefully, surprised by her own hearty appetite. Usually she could not eat when she was nervous, and the passing of a second night without rescue had made her very nervous indeed.

"This will be our last meal like this," said Mark.

Everyone looked up at him. "Do you think we'll be rescued today?" asked Katie.

"That's not what I mean. This will be the last time we use the food I brought along. From now on, we're going to live off the land."

Heather made a face. "What are we going to eat? Bugs?"

"How about fish?" said Mark. "They were jumping all over that stream yesterday. I brought enough tackle to get three lines in the water."

"I only like fish sticks," complained Heather. "Real fish is yucky."

"You've never had it cooked over an open fire," said Mark. "It's terrific. You'll love it."

84

"No, I won't."

Katie swallowed a spoonful of oatmeal, ignoring a nervous twinge in her stomach. She was becoming more suspicious all the time. It bothered her that Mark had laid out such an elaborate camp for them, not the temporary shelter she would have expected. Now he was conserving their supplies. Was he getting ready for a longer stay than he had predicted?

Katie waited almost an hour for a chance to ask him without the girls near enough to hear.

"It just makes sense to be careful," he answered. "With this rotten weather, we might be stranded for days before any planes can fly out to us. I'd rather have the canned food to fall back on, rather than use it all up and then be forced to hunt and forage."

Katie knew it made sense, but she still suspected that he knew more than he was telling her. She tried to put her suspicions aside while she washed the dishes, but they kept surfacing. Laurie brought the boughs from the trench and laid them on the campfire to burn while Mark cut new ones, and Heather grudgingly obeyed Mark's orders to help tidy up the site and put the breakfast supplies away. They were working together, but the tension underneath the surface was too powerful to lie still. Katie didn't know how long they could manage to live here together without an eruption.

Mark went back to the crippled *Adrian* and brought back a tackle box and three rods. He laid the poles aside and disappeared for a few minutes, returning with a long, sturdy stick. He fastened fishing line to it, fashioning a fourth rod.

Katie licked her lips. "Is that for me?"

"It's for Heather. I don't want her flinging hooks around until she's had some practice. Have you ever fished before?"

Katie shook her head.

"You're going to have all kinds of new talents when this is over."

He showed them all how to hunt for bait, a task that Katie found unsavory but was determined not to show.

She was aware of him watching her as she turned over rocks and dug in the ground, then stalwartly baited her own hook. She was surprised that it wasn't as bad as she thought it would be, and she began to feel proud of herself when she saw the approval on Mark's face.

Heather refused to let Mark teach her anything. She turned instead to Laurie, who took her sister a short distance down the shoreline and showed her how to hold the pole and watch the float for signs of nibbling fish.

Laurie was as experienced at fishing as she was at camping, and Katie once again felt envious of her expertise. She was also envious of the hours Laurie had spent alone with Mark to build those skills, and blushed at her own thoughts.

"So far so good, Reed," said Mark from behind her. "Can you march right out there and land a whale, or do you need some tutoring?"

Katie scrambled to her feet. "I've never used a reel before."

"I could have guessed that, since you've never fished before."

Mark strolled down the shoreline away from the girls, his rod in one hand and his rifle in the other. Katie noticed that he now carried it wherever he went, and she wondered if he was as worried about the bear as she was.

Mark set the rifle against a tree near the bank of the stream, then began to instruct Katie in the use of the rod and reel. With only a few practice flies, she was sending her line out in a smooth, flawless arc that looked very much like his own. He stood aside and watched, nodding in approval. Katie was pleased by her own quick learning and excited by his response to it, and let herself become so preoccupied by his presence that she didn't notice at first that her line had become heavy.

Mark did. "Bingo! Reel it in!"

Only then did Katie realize she had snagged the first fish of the day. She turned the crank of the reel carefully, trying to remember everything Mark had told her to do, and felt her excitement mounting with every turn. A flash of silver struck the surface of the water, then vanished beneath it.

"You got one!" shouted Heather.

"All right, Katie!" cheered Laurie.

Katie's rod bent sharply. She momentarily lost her balance, dizzied by the movement of the water around her, but recovered it at once. She didn't need Mark to steady her but he was there, his hands on her waist, not interfering with her movements and making no move to take over and haul the catch in himself.

"Bring it on home."

Katie braced herself and reeled the fish in. It flopped on the grass at her feet, sprinkling her shoes with flecks of water as it struggled and gasped.

"I'd guess seven pounds," Mark said. "That's a lot of breakfast right there. Good work."

"What'd you get?" called Laurie.

"I haven't the faintest idea," she called back.

"It's a small-mouth bass." Mark flipped the fish over. "Nice size, too."

Laurie and Heather both cheered. Heather scrambled up the bank to see it for herself, careful to keep her distance from her father. She inspected the fish with her wide blue eyes, then whooped and squeezed Katie. "Wow!"

"Let's get those lines in the water," said Mark. "Katie's making us look like a bunch of amateurs."

"I'm gonna get one too!" promised Heather, and she hurried back to her own pole. Laurie had already sent her flawlessly-cast line into the rapidly flowing water and was winding the reel slowly, feeling for a tug.

Katie was so pleased she found herself grinning, not only at her unexpected success but that Mark had, for the first time, called her by her first name instead of the formal, slightly insulting "Reed." She bent to detach the fish from the hook. Mark seemed surprised, as if he had expected her to delegate this part of the job to him. Katie baited the hook again, feeling very smug, but before she was finished Heather began screeching and jumping.

Mark dived for his rifle, but Katie's hand shot out to stop him. "It's not a bear," she pointed out. "It's a fish."

Heather had caught her first bass. She clapped her hands as she danced in excitement, her rich little voice rising in triumphant laughter. It was the first display of joy Katie had seen from her, and it erased the hardness and hostility from her face and revealed her as angelic and delicate as a pretty six-year-old should be. Laurie had taken the makeshift pole and was trying to remove the fish from the hook, but Heather didn't wait. She raced back to Katie and caught her in another explosive hug. "I did it! I did it! I caught a fish!"

"I saw it," said Katie, "and it's wonderful. You did it all by yourself!"

"I'm going to eat it for lunch!" she announced, fish sticks forgotten.

Katie praised her and hugged her back. Heather finally broke the embrace. "Gotta get another one!" She gulped, and was off to her pole again.

Katie turned to Mark but he was gone. She saw the rifle where he had left it, but she couldn't see him in the thick stand of pines and oaks framing the bank of the narrow stream. She looked around, expecting to see him emerge at any moment with a filet knife or his own fishing rod, but there was no sign of him. She felt a stab of disappointment, then maneuvered herself into the position he had shown her and sent her line back into the water.

Although Katie couldn't see him, Mark was watching her carefully. He had climbed a dozen feet or so up the side of the steep crag that rose sheerly on the edge of the stream, and had perched on a thick exposed arm of rock. From his vantage point he could see all three of them, Heather fishing impatiently, jerking her line out of the water every few seconds to look for her next triumph, Laurie expertly drawing in her line and landing a sizable fish herself, and Katie Reed, angling as if she had been doing it all her life. If there were such a magazine as *Family Fishing,* they could have been on the cover.

Mark propped his elbows on his knees and surveyed the scene below. Occasionally Katie would pause to look around for him, and he unconsciously held his breath, not wanting her to look up and see him. She was too sharp; he didn't want her to detect the sadness and longing that was welling up in him, and she surely would see it. She didn't miss much. She'd already figured out that he was hiding something. She'd know in a minute that he was dangerously close to shedding unaccustomed, unmanly tears.

Mark cleared his throat softly and concentrated on control.

Heather pranced below on the shore. He felt a lump in his throat as he watched her. She looked just like Laurie had at six, just as blond and petite, just as thrilled by her first fish. He could see her again, running to share her great news with Katie, but not with him. Even in her bubbling delight, she had coldly and deliberately closed him out.

Mark's deep hazel eyes left his younger daughter and moved to Laurie. She looked just as she had the last time they had camped together, although a year and a half had made her a little taller, a little more mature. She remembered his teaching well, using her experience to keep the camp running smoothly, showing Heather and Katie the ropes of camping, but this time without the warmth and closeness they had always shared before. He missed her. He missed them both.

And then there was Katie Reed.

She was everything he had wanted Adrian to be.

The one time Adrian had come camping, she had withdrawn with her sketch pad, frequently checking her watch to see when her ordeal would be over. But Katie was willing to pitch in and help. When Mark explained things to her, she listened, whereas Adrian had only sighed and tuned him out. Mark had enjoyed teaching Katie to fish; Adrian had refused to touch the pole or look at the bait. Mark had played out with Katie Reed the scene he had always imagined he would play out with Adrian, and Katie had responded with the enthusiasm he had wanted from his wife and never received.

The entire scene was an altered version of the one he

had longed for. His girls were here together, camping and fishing for the first time, as he had always planned, but Katie Reed was the ringer. She was in Adrian's place, fulfilling her role in this picturesque family tableau, cheering Heather's first fish, admiring Laurie's skills, and looking to Mark to teach and encourage her.

And he liked it. He liked her.

He liked the way she had climbed alone into a plane of which she was obviously terrified. He liked the way she coped with their emergency landing by handing her jacket back to Laurie, without panic, without begging for promises of survival. He liked the way she had attended to Heather's shock, putting aside her own shaken nerves to minister to his little girl's needs. He especially liked the way she had belted that wolverine. He liked the way she carried wood for the signal fire, baited hooks without wincing, and cast a line without hooking herself. He liked the way she saw right through him, and knew that he was lying to her about something.

What he didn't like was Katie Reed's faith.

It was the only thing that spoiled her, that reliance on prayer and the God she spoke to so freely. It was the only thing that prevented him from being truly glad that some accident of fate had sent her to help him with his children during this enforced ordeal. It was the only thing that kept Mark from allowing himself to enjoy the comfort of her presence.

That alien belief in a strange, capricious God had touched his life once before, and that was enough. He had seen its effect on a lonely, vulnerable person. He had felt the withering effects of relentless preaching. He had seen faith in God, Katie's God, drive a wedge into his marriage and destroy it completely.

He would never let Katie's God touch him again.

Mark felt his sadness passing, replaced now by the familiar edginess that boiled beneath the surface whenever he bothered to think about God. He deliberately detached his mind from the subject, slamming shut that huge, mental Bible that represented so much pain in his life. He let his eyes trail down over the stream again, and saw that Heather had finally tired of fishing and had gone to sit under the shade of an oak, rocking her princess doll with that funny name he could never remember. Katie was persistently casting her line in the water, but the only pile of fish that had grown was Laurie's. Mark couldn't count them from this distance, but she must have caught at least half a dozen. He smiled to himself; Laurie was certainly one of his. The smile faded when he remembered how much she hated him now.

Laurie had strung her catch, and as he watched her she picked up the fish and her rod and carefully crossed to the other side of the stream. She laid her catch at her feet and was about to cast her line when a sound made her head snap up. Katie heard it and whirled around at the same time.

Mark knew at once what it was.

The bear burst out of the thicket less than twenty feet from Laurie.

Mark didn't know which of the three screamed first, or loudest. He was on his feet, scrambling down the side of the craggy hill, cursing himself for leaving his rifle behind him. He half-ran, half-slid, sending trails of loose rock tumbling down around him. The clatter blended with the rumble of new thunder and the bawling roar of the bear and the echoing cries of his daughters.

Laurie had frozen at the sight of the beast. She could smell its musky scent and see the saliva dribbling from its jaws. She pitched back her head and shrieked. Over her own cry she heard Katie screaming at her to run, and with the automatic obedience of a well-trained child, she ran. She slipped and slid over the wet, muddy grass, dashing at random with no direction but forward, urged on by the crash of the heavy animal closing on her and Katie's voice shouting to her to keep going. She saw that her way would soon be blocked by the heavy growth of brush and thickets, and there was nowhere left to run but up the craggy hillside at the edge of the stream.

Mark slid to the bottom of the incline, off-balance, his horrified eyes riveted on Laurie and the monstrous beast behind her. "The gun!" he shouted. "Get the gun!"

Katie grabbed his rifle, and swung it to her shoulder. She pointed it in the general direction of the bear. Her finger stroked the trigger and the gun discharged, slamming the stock into her shoulder. The bear slowed, confused, searching for the source of the noise, but sensing no immediate threat took up the chase again.

The pause gave Laurie the time she needed to gain a foothold on the loose rock and pull herself upward on the incline. She climbed quickly, too terrified to look back. She struggled to pull herself upward, away from those yellowed, gaping teeth.

Mark finally reached Katie and grabbed the gun she thrust into his hands. He pulled it into his shoulder and swung it around, aiming at the bear but unable to aim accurately for the trembling of his arms and his own ragged breathing. The bear was climbing the hill only yards behind Laurie, and he was afraid of hitting her instead of the bear, and in those terribly long, short seconds of hesitation, Katie began to pray aloud, running after Laurie and the bear as if she were compelled by an unseen force. Her voice lifted above Laurie's screams and the thunder and the steady wail that was coming from Heather. Mark heard the name of God rolling through his head in Katie's voice, then in Heather's voice, and he squeezed the trigger and missed the mark widely. This time the bear did not even slow down.

Katie never broke stride, scooping rocks as she ran as if to pelt the bear, but it was too far above her. Only her voice could reach Laurie, and the girl heard it penetrate the din of her own strangled gasping.

"Save her, Jesus! Save her, Jesus!"

Laurie opened her mouth to scream and her own voice cried in unison with Katie's, "Save me, Jesus! Save me, Jesus!"

A large rock bounced and fell by her. Another followed, then another. Above Laurie's head there came a new sound, a new rumble, this time of rain-weakened rock giving way. The bear stopped, its head upright and alert, sensing the danger. More rock clattered down the hillside, first in a steady trickle, then suddenly in a constant downpour, rock after rock, piles of dirt rolling and ricocheting until the entire world was shaking.

The bear fled.

Laurie had grabbed onto a promontory of rock. Mark inched along the ledge, dodging flying stones as he reached out to his daughter. The rock broke loose under her hands, and Laurie started to fall, slipping backward down the hill with tons of rock raining down around her. She lifted her voice to cry one more time to Katie's God for salvation.

Her father's hands gripped her shoulders, then snaked around her waist. He swung her around and solidly planted her behind a lightning scarred stump of scrub pine, shielding them from the landslide with his body.

As suddenly as it had begun, the rockslide stopped.

A fine, misty drizzle began to fall while Mark slowly descended the rough hillside, stepping carefully on the loose piles of fallen rock. Laurie looked small in his arms, her pale blond hair spread over his shoulder and her enormous, frightened eyes staring back at the thicket. He carried her down to the stream, where the sight of her abandoned catch caused her to shudder and press closer to him.

"Katie," he called, "help me."

She was right beside him. "What is it?" She looked Laurie over quickly for signs of injury. "Is she hurt?"

"She's all right. Pick up the rifle. That bear could still be close by."

Katie took up the gun. "What about the fishing gear? Do you want me to get it?"

"No," said Mark quickly. "We'll come back for it later. I want us out of here, right now. Keep your eyes open and yell if you see anything move." He hefted Laurie in his arms and strode off in the direction of camp.

Heather hurried to catch up, her princess doll dangling from her left hand and her right hand reaching out to take hold of Mark's belt. For the first time they looked like a family, the three of them, coping together with their

93

shock and fright, sharing their relief that the crisis was over and Laurie was safe.

Katie watched them walking away from her and felt torn between joy and loneliness. She was warmed by the way they seemed to finally belong to each other, but she was also saddened by the crushing sensation of being left behind. She was not part of them, and their newfound unity left her feeling cut off and unneeded.

"That's silly," she said out loud. Of course it was. Whatever purpose God had had in mind when He sent her out here with this troubled family, it was not this. The only thing she knew for sure that she was supposed to do was to pray for them, and she had done so constantly since they had arrived here. Now she was seeing the fruit of those prayers, and she knew she should be glad for them, not fighting feelings of rejection. They were not her family.

Maybe now the rescue planes would come.

". . . your fault! You shouldn't have made us come out here!"

Heather's shrill voice snapped Katie's attention back to the family. She had caught up with her father, but instead of taking hold of him she swung her fist around and hit his back. She swung again, striking him with all the strength she had. Her moccasined foot flashed out and kicked his leg below the knee.

"It's all your fault that bear almost ate Laurie! You should have left us at Grandma's, where it's safe, and not made us come out here where bears'll get us and eat us! I hate you!"

Mark didn't slow down, but Katie saw his shoulders hunch, as if in defense against a heavy blow. Heather kicked him again, then sniffed in disgust and flounced back to Katie. The illusion of unity between them vanished and once again Katie could feel the dreadful need of this family to be made whole again. Heather reached up and took hold of Katie's arm, and Katie automatically hugged her. The child was hostile and angry, yet Katie sensed that there was more beneath her behavior than that.

94

Mark put Laurie down by the dead fire and began to rekindle it. "Katie, would you get a blanket?" he asked, a strangely civil request compared to his usual brusque orders. She set the rifle beside him and reached inside her tent, pulling out the first blanket she touched. She draped it over Laurie's shaking shoulders, and only then did she realize it was the blue plaid blanket that had upset Heather so much the first night they had slept here.

The fire leaped to life, and the aroma of burning wood smelled comforting. It was safe and normal. Mark was filling the coffee pot with water while Laurie watched him with dull eyes. He went over to the tall oak where their food stores were suspended and lowered the box.

Heather leaned against Katie. In spite of her ugly words, she seemed more vulnerable every moment.

Katie drew in a deep breath. "You really shouldn't talk to your father that way. Didn't you see the way he protected Laurie from the rockslide? We should all be grateful that he got to her in time to keep her from being hurt."

"I'm glad she's all right," said Heather, "but I still hate him."

"Why, Heather? What did he do that made you hate him so much?"

"He let Mommy die."

Katie's heart thumped. She recalled Heather's strange words in the airplane. "What do you mean by that?"

"He did it for the other one, the lady on the blue blanket. But he wouldn't do it for Mommy. He just went away. I'm going to hate him forever."

Mark hoisted the food box back up into the tree. Katie felt a raindrop splash on her hand. "Better get inside," said Mark. "Here comes more rain."

Heather trudged toward the tent. Katie wanted to ask her more questions, but she saw the wan-looking teenager slowly coming toward her, wrapped in the blue plaid blanket, and decided that the subject of Adrian McLaren's death could wait for a better time.

The rain dragged on until mid-afternoon. Mark brought hot chocolate and peanut butter and jelly sandwiches to the tent. "Don't worry," he said reassuringly, "I'll be out here riding shotgun on your lunch."

"Thanks, Daddy," said Laurie. They were the first words she had spoken since the attack.

Although Katie couldn't see Mark's face, she felt the catch in his voice when he answered, "You're welcome, honey."

Both girls dropped into an exhausted sleep after lunch. The rain slowed, then stopped, and Katie emerged from the tent to stretch her legs and breathe the freshly washed mountain air. The events of the morning had left her prickly with tension, but the cool, moist air refreshed her and she felt her nervousness slip away.

Mary Grace Kimball had told her that the mountains would be good for her . . . but she had been talking about the Glory Mountain Lodge and the Christian Singles Retreat. Katie smiled wryly at how the trip had turned out, and wondered what Mary Grace would say about it. Then her smile faded and she wondered if her friend knew yet that the plane she had personally arranged for Katie to fly in had gone down in the mountains. Katie hoped she didn't know, or else she might be afraid that Katie was dead.

How would Steve feel about it? Katie brushed her chestnut hair back from her face and thought about it. Would he care, knowing that the woman he had almost taken for his wife was lost in the northern Montana Rockies? Did he still care about her, or had her faith in the Lord so turned him off that he had lost all of his love for her? It seemed amazing to her that after a year of being together, he could suddenly change his mind about marriage. . . .

But he hadn't. When he gave Katie that choice to make, Steve or God, he had probably expected her to choose him. Maybe Steve had regretted his ultimatum after he had time to think about it. Maybe he had already tried to call her, wanting to put their love and their future back together again. Her phone might have been ringing all the time she was in the airplane with Mark and his daughters, ringing while they searched for a level strip of land to put down on after the engine had mysteriously failed.

Maybe that was why Mary Grace had insisted she make this trip, so she wouldn't be there to answer her phone!

The aroma of coffee interrupted her thoughts. Mark was standing beside her, offering her a cup. She took it gratefully, enjoying the warmth of the cup against her chilled hands. She had no gloves.

"I guess we'll start living off the land tomorrow," said Mark.

"Maybe we won't have to."

"Do you want to try fishing again today?"

"I meant we might be rescued by tomorrow."

Mark swished his coffee around in the cup. "It's going to rain again," he said. "When it finally quits, I'll set up some targets and teach you to use the rifle."

"Me? Why?"

"I need you to learn. I can't stay awake twenty-four hours a day, guarding the rest of you. Somebody has to take second shift, and I'd rather it was an adult and not one of two kids who hate me."

"I don't think they really hate you."

"They're putting on a very good act."

"I think they're still unsettled over losing their mother. That's not the same as hating you."

"Do they talk about her?"

"Sometimes. Not very much."

Mark looked at her questioningly.

Katie waved her free hand. "They just said that she was an artist, and very beautiful, and lots of fun to be with."

Mark nodded. "She was an artist, all right. Flighty, head in the clouds . . . changed her mind and her beliefs every other day. I used to think it was wonderful like the girls did, but after a while I got tired of it. They didn't. They always adored her."

Katie felt uncomfortable. She searched her feelings,

trying to figure out what was poking her, and was startled to realize it was jealousy. She could see Adrian: a tiny, fragile blond, stroking pastel ribbons of color across a canvas while her look-alike daughters watched, entranced. Katie had never been fragile, nor flighty, nor artistic, and it bothered her to think of these three people enchanted by a woman who was everything she was not.

"It was a lousy marriage," said Mark. "We shouldn't have done it at all, but Laurie was on the way. About the time we decided to quit, Heather was on the way, so we stuck it out. Please don't tell them that. They think Adrian was wonderful. I hope I didn't shock you."

"I don't shock that easily," said Katie.

"I'm grateful to you."

"To me? Why?"

"For firing that shot. It gave Laurie a head start on the bear. She wouldn't have been able to get away in time if you hadn't made the bear slow down. That's one crisis her mother would have been useless in. She wouldn't have picked up the gun at all, let alone had that lucky accident with it."

"It wasn't an accident."

"You mean you were trying to shoot the bear?"

"No . . ." Katie groped for words. "I mean, having that accident wasn't an accident."

"That's right, you people don't have accidents. Everything's an act of God, isn't it?"

Katie didn't like being referred to as one of "you people," as if she were some kind of freak. "It was this time."

"Next you'll be telling me that landslide was divinely inspired."

"It was."

"Come on, Reed. It rained all day yesterday and most of last night. The rain caused that rock to fall."

"At the very time and place you needed it to, right after three people prayed for a miracle to save Laurie, and then it stopped right after the bear ran away."

"I'm sure you're very sincere about this, but I've spent most of my life in mountains like these and nothing

98

happened out there today that doesn't happen every day."

"Like very convenient landslides."

"Nature. Just nature."

"Nature only does what God created it to do."

Mark didn't answer for a moment. He drained his coffee with a gulp. "You really think prayer made that rockslide start and stop?"

"I do."

"Well, if you believe that, then why didn't you rebuke that bear? Haven't you heard those stories in the circles you travel in? The ones about people who get attacked by charging bulls or sharks, and just tell them to go away in the name of Jesus? Why didn't you do that?"

Katie had heard such stories, and she felt surprised that Mark knew about them. She was also uneasy about the challenge it posed to her faith. Could she ever put her trust so radically in the power of God to order an attacking bear to go away?

"Maybe next time I will," she said lamely.

"Next time you'll know how to shoot something besides the breeze."

"Where did you hear stories about rebuking animals?"

"I've been around, Reed."

"I liked it better when you called me Katie."

Mark smiled. "Katie," he corrected himself. The smile faded, and his expression suddenly became serious. His deep hazel eyes searched her face. "Katie," he repeated softly.

She realized that he was going to kiss her. She put up a hand to stop him, but her hand kept moving until it was entwined in his hair and her other hand flew up around his neck. He tasted like coffee and gingersnaps, flavors she suddenly loved. She kissed him back, craving more, craving him. His arms came around her and he pulled her inside his open down vest, and she felt his heat warm her and become her own heat, until the chill of the air was gone and they were warm together.

Katie knew it was wrong. She told herself to let go and push him away before the time had passed when she could. He didn't want her—not Katie Reed. He was a man alone, and she was the only woman within hundreds of miles, and it had nothing to do with who she was or how he felt about her, but only that he was male and she was female. She tried to reason with herself and yet she still clung to him and moved with him, until she felt the pressure of his tongue and thought first of Steve, then of Mary Grace, then of Glory Mountain and God and remembered exactly who and what she was.

She wrenched free of him and pushed him with both hands, so violently that he stumbled backward and almost fell. "Hey! What happened?"

"I'm sorry . . . I'm sorry, but I can't—I'm not—"

"Okay, okay." Mark bent to pick up his fallen coffee cup and shrugged, a sheepish expression on his rugged face. "It must have been the coffee. It's a rare allergy that makes one man in every two million feel romantic at the wrong time. Sorry."

Katie felt foolish and was grateful for his joke to help cover it. "Better stick to hot chocolate, then."

"We've only got enough for a week, after that you're out of luck."

"I guess I'm lucky we won't be here for a week." Katie didn't feel lucky. She wanted more than anything to be back in his arms again.

"We might be."

"It can't rain for a whole week. The planes will come."

"The rain's got nothing to do with it."

Katie realized the joke was over. He was serious. "What did you say?"

Mark drew in a deep breath. "Look, Reed," he began, and Katie winced when he used her last name, "this is the way it is. I've got two angry, scared little girls, a wrecked airplane, and a prowling bear on my hands. I've got to have another adult around to help me. I can't be your father, too."

"I didn't ask you to be!"

"If anybody's looking for us, they're looking in the wrong place."

Panic hit her stomach. "What do you mean? Somebody must be looking for us!"

"If anybody heard my mayday call, yes. But they're still looking in the wrong place."

"But you gave directions! I heard you!"

"I gave the wrong ones."

"You . . . you what?"

Mark spread his hands helplessly. "Well, what could you expect? I never had an engine quit like that. I had both my kids in the plane with me. I was scared—I mean, I was *scared!* I misread the compass. Those things happen, Reed. I think I realized it as soon as I set down, but by then the radios were smashed and it was too late to do anything about it. I gave them a heading over a hundred miles from here. Even if they extend the search, they won't come this far north."

"Wait a minute—the flight plan. They'll check the flight plan, won't they?"

"I didn't file one. I hardly ever do, on short trips."

Katie's heart began to thump so hard it hurt. "What about the ELT? You showed me a radio and you said it would lead planes right to us!"

"It only works if there's a plane in the area to receive the signal. It has a limited range, and it runs on batteries. We can't turn it on until we hear a plane, or else we'll run down the batteries. It won't do us any good unless a plane flies over, and there hasn't been one since we got here. We're stuck, Reed. Nobody knows where we are."

CHAPTER 9

KATIE'S MIND WAS REELING BY THE TIME she reached the campsite. She ditched the dregs of her coffee and heard it hiss and pop as it splashed over the hot rocks ringing the fire. The aroma rose in the wet air and clashed with the sweet, piney fragrance of the rain-drenched woods. She could still taste Mark and gingersnaps, and she had never been so confused in her life.

Her response to Mark McLaren had shocked her. Never before, not even with Steve, had Katie felt such a yearning for any man's touch. Even now she felt the impulse to turn around and go back to him, to fling herself fully into the protection of his arms and give herself over to that wonderful feeling of being the center of his existence. She wanted with all her heart to believe that it was for this purpose alone that God had sent her aloft in a doomed airplane, so she could be divinely knocked out of the sky and planted in the remotest corner of the Great Divide with the one man God had chosen for her.

Hogwash.

She could hear Mary Grace Kimball's wavery voice speaking out above the sweet tones of the organ she always played during Katie's visits. *Hogwash, dear. The man doesn't know the Lord, and what you're feeling doesn't have much to do with the Lord, either. Quit trying on unequal yokes and start looking for the man God really has waiting for you. Look somewhere appropriate like Glory Mountain.*

Katie felt tears smarting her eyes, as if Mary Grace had been there to deliver the rebuke in person. She felt foolish and ashamed, especially after the disastrous outcome of her engagement to Steve. Hadn't she learned her lesson by now? Didn't she know better than to step out of God's backyard and go looking for love among the unsaved?

Her shame abruptly turned to anger. Why not? Why couldn't she open her arms and her life to Mark McLaren? It didn't have to make a difference that she was a Christian and he wasn't. Wasn't that what Steve had accused her of—being sanctimonious? Maybe he was right. No one was born Christian; Mark could learn from Katie. He could live with her and see her example and gradually accept the truth and turn his heart to God and . . .

Hogwash.

Mary Grace's imaginary voice rose in pitch to be heard above the organ. *You said exactly the same thing about Steve, and look what happened. You can't gamble so recklessly on the hope that a man will change. They never do. Stick to your own kind, Katie Reed. Christians only. Don't be a fool.*

"But I *am* a fool!" whispered Katie out loud. She dropped her tin cup beside the fire and watched it bounce on the damp earth. It struck the cup that Mark had used that morning and came to rest beside it, leaning slightly on the incline as if it were snuggling up. She curled her lip and inched the two cups apart with the toe of her shoe.

A stiff breeze rattled through the branches of the trees and sent a small shower of raindrops pouring down from the leaves. Katie shivered in the cold wind and longed again for the warmth of Mark's arms. She scanned the dark clouds stretching out infinitely across the sky and

103

felt a pang of fear rising out of her anger and distress. The last words Mark had spoken to her had jarred her more fundamentally than any prophecy of doom could have. They were lost.

The idea of being stranded hadn't frightened her as long as she had believed someone was trying to find them. Now that she knew the truth, she felt truly alone. It was as if the mountains around her had grown taller, thrusting their gray and purple peaks up around her like walls to hide her from the eyes of anyone who might be searching for them. Montana itself had stretched and grown out of its borders, dwarfing her into an invisible bit of dust.

She had never felt so small.

From the back of her mind came the reminder that she should pray. Katie knew she should, but her mind would not focus and keep still. She didn't know whether to lift up her ridiculous, unholy love for Mark McLaren or her utter terror at being stuck out in the middle of the wilderness with no hope of rescue. She fought to keep her thoughts in line and struggled to form the words of prayer. Only one word formed: Jesus.

She stood still, speaking the name.

"Where can I go from your Spirit? Where can I flee from your presence? If I go up to the heavens, Thou art there; if I make my bed in the depths, you are there. . . ."

It was Laurie's voice, coming from the tent.

The familiar words of Katie's favorite psalm rolled over her like a healing balm. She felt her fears quiet until even the bear seemed to fade away like a bad dream. She felt a peace descend over her heart, that wonderful peace that passed all understanding, and she knew beyond any doubt that she could not be lost as long as the Lord knew where she was.

"Thank you," she said gratefully.

Laurie's head jerked upright when Katie entered the tent. She looked like a little girl who had been caught reading in bed after lights-out, with her large, five-cell flashlight trained on Katie's open Bible. Heather was less

104

surprised, but her deep blue eyes were so steadily fixed on Katie that she felt a sensation of guilt, as if the imprint of Mark's lips was stamped across her own.

Laurie snapped off the light. "I hope you don't mind," she said quickly. "I finished my book and we were getting kind of bored."

"You can use my Bible any time you want to."

Heather smiled triumphantly. "See? I told you she wouldn't get mad."

"We were just reading some stories," Laurie said, laying the Bible back on Katie's sleeping bag.

"Any story in particular?"

"Where's David and Goliath?" asked Heather. "We couldn't find it."

Katie turned to the story and began to read it out loud. Laurie turned the flashlight back on, its brilliant light piercing the gloom of the tent and glowing on the page. Katie took the flashlight in her hand, and Laurie rolled over onto her back with her eyes closed, listening. When Katie was finished, she said, "I didn't remember that part about him killing bears that attacked his sheep."

"Lions, too," said Heather.

"I don't care about lions," Laurie sighed. "I care about—"

"About what, Laurie?" urged Katie.

"Did God really save me from that bear?"

The question caught Katie off guard. She could sense Laurie's eyes boring through the murkiness of the tent. Katie could see how serious she was, and yet she could hear Mark saying, "Don't go filling her head with all that religious talk. Leave her alone." For a moment Katie wavered, not wanting to go against Mark's command, but she could feel the intensity of Laurie's need for answers and didn't feel that she could withhold them.

"You can tell us," said Heather, as if reading her mind. "We won't tell *him*."

"Dad doesn't want us to talk about the Bible," said Laurie. "But I'm not asking him, I'm asking you. Did God save me from that bear?"

Katie had denied the Lord once when she fell in love

105

with Steve. She had denied him a second time, minutes ago, when she allowed herself to be pulled into the arms of another non-Christian. She would not deny him three times.

"Yes, Laurie. He did."

"Wasn't it just a coincidence?"

"Do you think it was?"

"No," said Laurie, and sat up. "I know it wasn't. I feel it, somehow. I know."

Katie nodded. "That's the work of the Spirit, Laurie. He lives in us to tell us that the Word of God is true."

"Why did he save me? Was it because you asked him to?"

"Maybe because *you* did."

"So did I," added Heather, wanting her credit too.

Laurie twisted a strand of hair. "Why would he want to do anything for me? I'm not one of those born-again people."

Katie was surprised to hear her say "born again."

Laurie read the surprise on her face. "Somebody used to talk to me about it, and I almost did it once, but then my mother got sick and everything got so mixed up. . . ."

"And you were angry with God, weren't you?"

It was Laurie's turn to be surprised. "How did you know?"

"I've been mad at him, too." Katie related her own story, skipping many of the details but still outlining honestly the year she had spent planning her wedding, before she let her faith in God take over and send her one great love out of her life.

"And you still believe in him?"

"God didn't leave me, Laurie. I left him. It was hard to accept that, but now I'm glad that he stopped me before I made a terrible mistake with my life. If I had stayed close to him and followed his Word in the first place, I wouldn't have wasted that year with Steve and set my heart on a life that wasn't right for me."

Laurie thought it over. "After everything that happened with Mom, then Dad going off leaving us . . . it's hard to think that God really cares about me."

Katie turned to Psalm 139. The words of love and reassurance rolled off her lips from memory. Katie hugged the Bible to her heart as she spoke them, remembering the first time she had read them and realized how intimately God knew and loved her. The glow on Laurie's face told her that she was experiencing the same thing right now.

Heather's face had clouded over when Katie spoke the verse about being woven together in the womb, and she withdrew to her own thoughts.

Laurie's face lost its glow when Katie finished the psalm: "Search me, O God, and know my heart; test me and know my anxious thoughts. See if there is any offensive way in me . . ."

"Katie?"

"Yes?"

"Does that mean God doesn't love us when we hate people? Even if it's just one person? Is that one of those offensive ways he's talking about?"

Katie took a breath, trying to frame an answer. "God never stops loving us, Laurie, and he wants us to love each other. When we don't do that, we disobey his Word and that cuts us off from him. We can always choose between obeying or disobeying, and when we choose to disobey, we shouldn't be surprised that God seems far away from us. It isn't that he leaves us—we leave him. But he never stops loving us."

"Can I be born again even if I hate my father?"

"I don't think you hate your father. I think you're very hurt and angry, but that's because you love him, not because you don't."

"I don't love him," said Heather sullenly.

"I was sure I hated him."

"The way you talk about him? And look at him? And act like him? Laurie, you're crazy about him."

Laurie shot Katie a shy smile that told her she was right.

"No, she doesn't!" protested Heather. "We hate him, and we always will forever and ever!"

"He shouldn't have left us when Mom died," said Laurie.

"He knows that, honey. That's why he came back and why he brought you out here. In his own way, he's trying to say he's sorry and make up for lost time."

"I don't care if he's sorry," said Heather. "He can't get us back. Not ever."

"And he loves you very, very much, Laurie."

"What do I do, Katie? I can't help how I feel."

"You can forgive him."

"What if I can't?"

"You can. You don't have to feel forgiving toward him. Just make the decision to forgive him and start acting like you have. God will give you the feelings later."

"Really?"

Heather sat up. "Don't do it, Laurie."

"If I forgive Dad for going away, can I be born again like you?"

"Any time you want to."

"We don't want to!" snapped Heather.

"I do," said Laurie.

Heather watched in angry silence while Laurie bowed her head and haltingly spoke the words that would change her life. She must have heard them before. Katie wondered who had spoken to this girl about the Lord.

Her mother?

Possibly. Adrian's untimely death would have given Laurie's flimsy hold on faith a deadly blow. It would certainly explain why Mark was hostile to God, if he had seen his devout young wife die without miraculous intervention. Katie opened her arms and Laurie came into them, crying softly with relief, and Katie held her tight, feeling as if she were both mother and sister to her.

"When will I feel different?"

"Soon."

"No, you won't!" said Heather. "You really hate him like me. You can't love him anymore because he let Mommy die!"

Laurie blotted tears from her cheeks. "Why do you keep saying that? Mom had cancer. We told you that."

Katie was surprised by the relief she felt. If Adrian

McLaren had died of cancer, then Mark couldn't be responsible.

"It doesn't matter what she had. He did it for the lady on the blue blanket but he didn't do it for Mommy. He went away and he didn't come back."

"Katie!" called Mark from outside. "Open the flap, would you?"

Katie hesitated, wanting to hear Heather out, but the child turned her back at the sound of her father's voice. Katie obeyed, aware of the excitement she had begun to feel and dismayed because she knew it was coming from Mark's closeness.

He shoved the ELT inside. "I've got a leak in my tent," he explained. "We can't afford to let this get wet. It's our ticket out of here."

"We'll take good care of it," said Katie.

Mark hesitated. "Everybody okay in there?"

Katie knew he was asking about her. After he had told her the truth about the mayday call, she had left him without a word. He probably thought she was still upset.

"We're all fine," she said. She tasted gingersnaps and felt a warm thrill hum through her body and vibrate on her lips.

"Great. Target practice in five minutes."

"For who?"

"You, Reed. I need a good night's sleep for a change."

"I'll be right out," Katie automatically began to smoothe her hair, then caught herself. She was learning to shoot a rifle, not going on a date. She shoved the ELT over near Heather's sleeping bag.

"What's that thing?" asked Heather, her voice still sulky.

Katie quickly explained what the ELT was, careful not to give away any hint that the planes it was supposed to signal would not be coming within range. Not without luck. Not without a nudge from God.

"Do you mind if I use your Bible a while, Katie?" asked Laurie.

"As long as you like."

"I think Dad's starting to like you."

Katie glanced at her, startled. "Why?"

"He called you Katie."

"He called her Reed," retorted Heather.

"But he called her Katie first," persisted Laurie. "Didn't you hear him?"

"I didn't notice," lied Katie, and crawled out of the tent.

Heather put down her doll and scowled at her sister. "You didn't really mean all that stuff, did you?"

"Yes, I did. I've been thinking about it for a long time."

"You never told me."

"I didn't think you'd understand."

"You aren't going to forgive him, are you?"

"I'm trying."

"Laurie!"

"I can't explain it. I just know I want things to be different. Don't you?"

"All I want is to go home to Grandma's."

"Well, you can't do that until they come and rescue us, so you might as well try to get along with Dad."

Heather stroked her princess doll's golden hair. Laurie turned back to Katie's Bible. Later, when Laurie wasn't looking, Heather reached over to the transmitter and switched it on.

"It's our ticket out of here," she told her doll. "We're going to go home, and not even God can make me love him again."

CHAPTER 10

KATIE DROPPED A BUNDLE OF WOOD on the pile and gauged it carefully. It was enough to last until tomorrow morning. She panted from exertion and saw her breath misting in the cold air. Above her, the stark mountains stood rigid, like giant bear teeth, their peaks glistening with a thick layer of snow.

There was no doubt about it: it was getting colder.

Mark and his daughters had started wearing sock caps pulled down over their ears. Heather had refused at first, because the caps were identical, but the cold wind soon turned her eartips red and her protests turned to grudging cooperation. Mark had produced from his pack a thick maroon hooded sweatshirt for Katie, and she was amazed by the difference it had made. She pulled the warm hood up over her chestnut hair and knew Mark was right when he said most of one's body heat was lost through the top of the head. She wore the sweatshirt day and night, pulled over the top of her own sweaters, which were worn over one of Mark's T-shirts. If it got much colder, she'd wind up wearing his whole wardrobe.

But it couldn't get much colder. If it did, they would all be in serious trouble.

Ten days had passed with no sign of an airplane. The

signal fire lay ready and waiting, protected from the rain and wind by the tarp they had stretched over the top. The ELT was dry and undisturbed, nestled between Laurie's sleeping bag and Heather's. All they needed now was for someone to come looking for them. But no one had.

Katie shivered and pulled the sleeves of the sweatshirt down over her hands. She stood by the fire, absorbing the warmth, and glanced over at the rifle propped up on the woodpile. It was heavier than she had expected, and after her first night of guard duty she had abandoned carrying it in favor of staying near enough to grab it quickly. The responsibility of guarding Mark and his daughters was as heavy as the rifle, and Katie checked her watch for the third time in five minutes, anxious for the time when Mark would wake up and come to relieve her.

Mark was prompt. She heard his tent flap opening five minutes before the time she would have called him. Katie fed another handful of sticks to the fire, concentrating hard to keep from turning around too quickly. Mark's presence excited her more than she liked to admit.

"Nippy, isn't it?" he greeted her.

"Nippier every night." She poured coffee into a tin cup and handed it to him. "I've been wanting to ask you a question."

Mark sipped coffee and sighed. "I hope it's not one of those heaven-or-hell types. I'm not in the mood."

"Why don't we just walk out of here?"

"Because it's a bad idea."

"Why? There haven't been any planes at all. It doesn't make any sense for us just to sit here in the middle of nowhere while they're looking for us in the wrong place."

"It makes more sense than walking out."

"Why?"

"It's almost impossible for pilots to spot people on the ground, especially if they're surrounded by woods like we are. As long as we've got this open space, the signal fire, and the wreckage of the plane, we're much better

112

off. Our chances of being seen are greater here than if we were out there somewhere on foot."

"What good does it do us to be visible if there's no one to see us?"

"It's too dangerous to try walking out with the girls. Walking across terrain like this isn't like strolling down Main Street. On this rough ground there's always the danger of tripping and falling. A sprained ankle or broken leg would really set us back. We can't deal with a serious injury out here."

"We could tell the girls to be very careful."

"Careful of what? You don't always see the loose rocks or roots before you fall over them. One badly placed step could result in a turned ankle or a sprain. Besides, we'd have to carry the tents and equipment with us, and that's just too great a load for the four of us. We couldn't leave anything behind because we'd need it as soon as we stopped to make camp. It can't be done, not safely at least."

"But we've got to do something!"

"That's a natural reaction. When you get stranded, you've always got a strong urge to do something about it. It's against human nature to sit tight and wait for help to come. But that's what we've got to do."

"Help isn't coming."

"Strange comment for you to make."

Katie looked away quickly. He was right. She should be more confident, believing that God had sent them here for a purpose and was guiding them along. Her own wavering faith bothered her. She was losing her struggle with fear. Even though she kept reminding herself that God knew exactly where they were, she saw the worried glances Mark kept giving the snow on the peaks. The concern in his eyes sent shivers through her body. He knew they were running out of time. More than once Katie had longed to wrap her arms around him and let him comfort her, but she always managed to regain her control before giving in to those impulses.

She felt Mark's hand on her shoulder. "They'll keep looking for us."

"For how long?"

"Don't panic, Katie. They'll find us."

Katie. He rarely used her first name. She thought quickly of the first time she had heard him say it and the fragrance of gingersnaps whirled in her memory. His fingers touched her neck and she shuddered. It would be so easy to turn around and lean against him. . . .

"I won't panic," she said firmly. "God knows where we are."

Mark dropped his hand. "Go get some sleep."

Katie turned immediately and headed for the girls' tent. The stinging wind hit her forcefully and brought tears to the corners of her eyes.

Mark hadn't said anything about that rainy afternoon when he had kissed her. He acted as though it had never happened, which probably made life easier but still bewildered and hurt her. His impersonal attitude toward her was an insult; how could he have so easily put their embrace out of his mind when it occupied her thoughts day and night? Had it been such a meaningless thing to him?

She entered the tent and crept into the sleeping bag, huddling under the covers until she began to feel warm again.

The Glory Mountain Singles Retreat had been over for four days. By now her family knew she was missing. Her mother would have called Mary Grace, trying to find out if Katie had changed her plans. Her father would have telephoned the lodge, looking for her. Katie felt a pang of sadness, knowing how worried they must be. Her parents must have been panic-stricken to learn that Katie had never arrived at Glory Mountain. And how must Mary Grace feel? She had arranged the trip and insisted Katie go.

Did Steve know? Did he even care?

Katie tried to imagine him learning the news, but couldn't. The last ten days of her life had made an entire year with Steve fade away, until it seemed to be a complete waste of time.

That might be the purpose for this time of marooning:

114

to get over Steve. Katie certainly felt as if her knowledge of life had expanded. It came from the constant vigilance they were all forced to keep, watching out for predators. The bear had not returned, although Mark had twice found its tracks near the camp. They had resumed fishing, always under the protection of Mark's loaded rifle, and their patience rewarded them with meals of small-mouth bass, white perch, and landlocked salmon. Mark had shot a rabbit, but Heather refused to touch it and Katie found the unfamiliar taste gamey and strange. Only Laurie had dug in, her gusto for the outdoors making Katie feel narrow and sheltered.

Laurie stirred in her sleep. Katie listened to her gentle breathing and felt another pang of guilt. If they were all stranded here because God wanted to teach Katie a lesson, was it Katie's slowness to learn that was keeping them all here?

Katie went to sleep praying for guidance and trust.

Morning brought no relief from the cold.

Katie knelt and poked at the fire with a stick. It blazed back to life and she extended her hands to warm them. She wished it were evening instead of morning: she longed for the warmth of the sleeping bag again. It was the only place she felt truly comfortable.

Except for that brief time she had been in Mark's arms.

"Will you *stop* it?" she said impatiently to herself. "Don't even think about it anymore!"

"Don't think about what?" asked Laurie from behind her. Katie turned around, embarrassed, and tried to think of an answer. She didn't have a chance to say anything. A scream split the air.

"Heather!" they both cried at once. Katie looked around wildly for the child. Laurie ran off toward the stream, searching. The scream repeated, vibrating on the thin, cold air. Katie's mind spun. Had the bear come back? Where was Mark? Where was the rifle?

"Katie! Katie!"

Katie spun around. Heather was running toward her, her legs pumping, her face white with terror. "Where's Laurie? Did the bear get her? Where's Laurie?"

Laurie had heard her and turned back. "Heather! Oh, thank God!"

"Katie!" Heather reached her and hugged her waist. "What is it? Who's screaming?"

"I don't know, honey. We thought it was you."

They heard it a third time, and this time it sounded closer. There was an unhuman quality to it, an earthy, feral undertone they hadn't heard before. "It's an animal," said Katie, dropping her voice.

"Where?" asked Heather. "What is it?"

"I don't know. It's somewhere close. Come back to the fire."

"Katie!" It was Mark. "Are the girls with you?"

His voice brought reassurance, the promise of safety. "We're all here!" she called back. A moment later she saw his red sock cap flash between the trees. He came into the camp quickly, counting heads to make sure they were all accounted for.

"What is it?" asked Katie unsteadily.

"It's a mountain lion."

"Lion?" Heather went rigid. "A lion?"

"Don't worry, Heather. As long as we mind our own business it won't bother us."

"What's it doing around *here?*"

"Hunting. Mountain lions hunt along a regular route. It may hang around for a day or two, and then it'll be gone. We'll just stick close to camp until it leaves. No problem."

"That's what you said before we crashed!"

"We didn't crash. We landed. If you forget everything else, at least remember that."

Laurie stuck her hands in her vest pocket. "Are mountain lions dangerous to people?"

"They can be. Don't walk up to it and say hello."

"Are you kidding?" Katie crouched by the fire, fumbling for the coffee pot. Her hands shook.

"Don't worry, Katie," said Laurie in a conspiratorial whisper. "David beat lions off the sheep, too."

"David who?" asked Mark.

"Never mind," said Laurie.

116

Mark looked confused for a moment, then his face hardened. "Oh, that." He shot Katie a disapproving scowl. She ducked under it, as if he had slung a rock at her.

They didn't hear the mountain lion again that day, although Mark was especially vigilant during meal times. He stood with his rifle in his hands and his gaze sweeping the perimeter of the camp while Katie cooked the perch filets.

It screamed twice during Katie's early-night watch. She abandoned the warmth of the fire to sit outside Mark's tent, the rifle balanced across her lap. Both times Mark called out to ask her if she was all right; both times she answered, "Of course I am," feeling foolish because he knew she was hovering near him.

The next day Mark found its kill.

It had brought down a mule deer. Mark whistled at the size of it. "There's got to be two hundred pounds of deer here," he said to Katie. "That's a big mountain lion."

Katie was surprised to find grass and leaf scrapings covering the carcass. "That's how they mark their kill," Mark explained. "If the mountain lion was finished, it would have left the deer uncovered so other animals could feed on it. The covering shows that it isn't finished feeding yet, and plans to come back later for more."

"I didn't know about that."

"Nature's very efficient. Only people waste food. We're probably the most useless creatures in the food chain."

"I'm just glad we're at the top of it."

"Thinking about the bear?"

"And this mountain lion. I'm starting to feel a little like prime rib."

Mark grinned for the first time in days. "After all the fish, I'm tempted to take a bite out of you."

"Fish is really better for you."

"But not as much fun." Mark moved away from the deer. "Let's get out of here before the lion gets hungry again."

Laurie and Heather had kept their distance, Laurie out of fear of the mountain lion and Heather from disgust. "I hate mountain lions," said Heather. "They shouldn't hurt cute little deers."

Mark stepped over a half-rotted log. He reached out his hand to help Katie over it. Even with two pairs of socks on, her toes were tingling in the cold. She scanned the sky again. No sign of planes. Twelve days now. She thought about her family and Mary Grace, and sighed. Then she realized Mark had not let go of her hand.

"Mountain lions eat deer," Laurie told Heather. "If they didn't, they'd starve. That's the way nature is."

"I hate nature, too," groused Heather.

"I like nature," Mark said softly to Katie. He stopped suddenly, and waited until the girls were several yards ahead before he turned to Katie. "There's a lot to be said for nature."

His hand tightened around hers. Katie was mesmerized by his eyes. "Don't you think so?" he asked, his lips almost touching hers.

Katie fought with herself. "It looks dangerous to me."

"Sometimes it is. Sometimes it's very nice," he answered, and brushed her lips with his.

Katie quivered in every fiber of her body. For more than a week she had dreaded a moment like this. For more than a week, she had longed for it. She pulled her head back before he could kiss her again.

"Dad!"

Mark jerked upright, pulling the rifle up to his shoulder.

Laurie was thirty feet ahead of them, jumping up and down, pointing toward the sky. "Dad! There's a plane! A plane!"

Mark gaped at the sky, then groped backward for Katie's hand. "Get back to camp! Turn on the transmitter!"

Laurie broke into a run. Heather hustled after her. "We're going home! We're going home!"

"What about the fire?" asked Katie. "Should we go light it?"

"Not yet. The transmitter will let them know we're around here. We'll save the fire until the chopper gets here."

"Why do you think they'll send a chopper?"

"No one in his right mind would try to land a plane around here."

"You did."

"Cheap shot, Katie." He let the rifle slide to the ground and took both her hands in his. "Looks like you finally got your wish. We'll be out of here in no time. Does that make you happy?"

"Yes," she said quickly. The truth was, she didn't know. The sound of the plane's engine filled the air, a sound she had so often taken for granted back home in Helena and missed so terribly out here in the mountains. It was a sound that brought relief, knowing that her ordeal was finally over and she would soon be home, warm and comfortable again. Her family and friends would be told she was alive, and she could pick up the pieces of her life and go on.

Without Mark.

Rescue meant the end of Mark. The thought sent waves of pain spiralling through her body, down her arms, and into the hands he held tightly in his own.

He pulled her hands around his waist. "Are you going to try to patch things up with old what's-his-name?"

"Of course not. That's all over now."

Mark grinned broadly. "Then what are you doing Saturday night?"

Katie didn't know if he was teasing her and she struggled to find something to say, but it was too late and Mark's mouth had ground down on hers. The hum of the plane's engine intensified until her head was ringing with the roar and she thought the plane was going to land right beside them. It was time to go home and time to leave Mark, and the prospect sent her arms around his waist and every sensible thought vanished. Something new and unfamiliar awakened in Katie's heart, and all the while she drowned in the gingersnap sweetness of his kiss she gripped her hands together behind him and whispered all

119

the words she could not say. The roar diminished and faded away as the plane flew off, lost to sight above the tops of the pines that jutted up like monstrous Christmas trees, perfuming the air with a wintry fragrance that would forever blend with coffee and gingersnaps in Katie's feverish memory.

She thought she heard the plane returning, but the hum of the engine sounded strangely like a growl this time. Mark broke away from her and grabbed the rifle. Katie opened her eyes; the sunlight blinded her. She winced in sudden pain, then focused on a tawny cougar crouched above her on the rocks. Its eyes were wild, huge green and gold orbs with pinprick pupils.

"Get behind me!"

Katie stepped back numbly.

"Walk slowly—*slowly*—to the camp. Don't make any sudden moves . . . just get going. Slowly! Get going."

Katie moved hypnotically, her eyes on the cougar. Its head twitched and jerked as those enormous, wild eyes followed her. Mark backed away from it, rifle held high and ready. The cougar growled savagely, leaped off the rocks in the opposite direction and sped away toward its kill.

Katie could no longer walk slowly. She ran toward the camp. She heard Mark's boots thudding behind her, heard them slow and stop, heard his voice telling her that the cougar was gone and they were safe. She slowed down to a walk, trying to get control of her runaway terror before the girls saw her.

Laurie emerged from the tent just as Katie came into camp. The look on the girl's face stopped her cold.

"Laurie? What's the matter?" asked Katie, gasping from the racing of her own heart.

Laurie looked beyond Katie to her father. "Dad, you'd better take a look at the transmitter. I think something's wrong."

Mark handed Katie the rifle and dived into the tent. Heather came out at once, not wanting to be near him. She clutched her princess doll to her chest.

"What happened to the transmitter?" asked Katie.

"I don't know. I kept flipping the switch but there wasn't any power."

"When is the plane coming back?" asked Heather. "Will we get to Grandma's house today?"

Mark burst out of the tent. He tore down the hill toward the signal fire. He fought with the knots but couldn't loosen them. He yanked off his deerskin gloves and threw them to the ground, struggling with his bare fingers to pry the knots open and free the tarp. Laurie ran after him, but stopped a few yards away.

"The plane's gone, Dad."

"It might come back. Help me with this!"

Laurie quickly untied one end of the tarp. It fluttered in the brisk wind. Mark freed the other side and pulled out a thin stick that had been cut to raise thin strips of wood along its length. He fumbled in his vest pocket and pulled out a lighter. The stick ignited and began to burn steadily. Mark held it poised, above the pyramid of wood, watching the sky and listening.

The plane did not return.

Mark and Laurie waited almost an hour before silently pulling the tarp over the top of the signal fire. Mark fastened the last of the knots and picked up a few sticks of wood to carry back with him. He would carve them tonight, feathering them until they became ready-to-light torches. They would be stored in the edges of the signal mound, ready to light at a moment's notice, if another plane were to appear in the sky.

If.

Katie was seated by the campfire with Heather leaning against her. She didn't speak when Mark and Laurie came into camp. Their grim faces shadowed their disappointment. Mark glanced at the thick snow on the mountain peaks, and worry rutted the lines around his mouth.

"What happened to the transmitter?" he demanded.

"Is it broken?" asked Katie.

"Broken? No—the battery's dead! It was all right when I put it in your tent. What happened to it?"

"I don't know."

"The battery wouldn't discharge by itself! Did you touch it? Did you turn it on?"

"No," answered Katie feebly. She withered under his accusing glare.

"Laurie?"

"No, Dad. I never touched it."

All eyes turned toward Heather.

"When is the plane coming back?" she asked.

"Heather," said Mark steadily, "did you turn on the transmitter?"

She nodded. "I called that plane to come and get us. I want to go home to Grandma's. When is it coming back?"

Mark threw the wood down. It clattered against the stones ringing the fire.

"It isn't coming back! You ran down the battery! That plane flew right over and never knew we were here because you ran down the battery!"

Heather's eyes widened. Her doll slipped from her fingers and landed in the dirt with a dull thump.

"Mark," cautioned Katie, "she didn't know any better. She thought she was helping."

"What good does that do? We're stuck out here because of her! That plane's long gone by now, and if it was a search plane, the pilot will report a negative finding here. That was our one chance to get out of here, and now it's gone!"

CHAPTER 11

"I DIDN'T MEAN TO BREAK THE RADIO! I didn't mean it!" Heather had sobbed those words so many times her voice had become hoarse. Katie didn't know what to do but what she had been doing for more than an hour now, holding her close and shaking her every time the child began to become hysterical. Heather refused to be comforted. She huddled in Katie's arms and cried piteously, clutching her doll and squeezing her eyes closed every time she glimpsed the dead, useless ELT beside her sleeping bag.

"We know you didn't, Heather," Katie said again. She had crooned those words over and over, but they had no effect. "We know you were trying to help us all get home. You just didn't understand."

"I don't want to stay here anymore! I want Grandma!"

"We'll go home, Heather. The plane will come back."

"What if it doesn't? What if we have to stay here forever?"

Katie stroked the child's damp and matted hair and thought of the worried expression on Mark's face whenever he saw the thickening snow on the mountains. At least Heather had no concept of the danger that lay ahead as winter approached. She wasn't worried about survival.

"We won't, honey. The plane will come back, and your father will light the signal fire. We'll be fine."

"I don't want to stay here with him!"

Katie watched Heather's hands squeeze the princess doll's soft body. "It isn't so bad. Your father is taking very good care of us."

"I don't want to be with him! Grandma says he wants us back but I don't want to live with him anymore."

"Heather, I know you were very hurt when he left you, and sometimes it's hard for children to understand why grown-ups do things they shouldn't do. Your father loves you very much, Heather, and he never stopped loving you, even while he was away. He just needed time to be alone . . . it was hard for him to lose your mother, and—"

"He didn't have to lose her! He could've saved her but he didn't do it! He did it for the other one, but he wouldn't do it for Mommy!"

"Do what, Heather?"

"Kiss her alive."

"Kiss her alive? I don't understand."

"Like Sleeping Beauty."

Katie felt excitement stirring in her heart. She was beginning to understand why Heather hated her father, and it was so simple she was amazed that she hadn't seen it before.

"Heather, Sleeping Beauty is only make-believe. There's no such thing as a kiss back to life. That only happens in fairy tales. Your father couldn't kiss your mother back to life. It's impossible."

"No it isn't. He did it for the lady on the blue blanket."

The blue blanket. Katie's mind raced. What had Laurie said about that blue blanket?

A woman. A woman in an automobile accident. They had brought her into the house and laid her on that blue blanket . . .

"Did Heather see her?"

"Yeah. She was real scared, especially when the lady's heart stopped."

"She died?"

"Dad did mouth-to-mouth and she was okay after that."

Mouth-to-mouth.

Katie jerked upright, realizing.

Mark was a paramedic. Heather had seen him perform CPR and her little girl's imagination had confused it with the fairy tale kiss of the charming prince.

"Oh, Heather!" exclaimed Katie. "Now I understand what you mean!"

Heather sniffled. "That's why I don't ever want to love him again. He let Mommy die."

"Oh, no, Heather. You don't understand." Katie tried to explain CPR to her in the simplest words she could find. Heather at first looked surprised, then interested, but her face fell back into its sorrowful lines and she held the princess doll tightly against her cheek.

"But he didn't do it for Mommy."

"It wouldn't have made any difference, Heather," said Katie gently. "In the fairy tales, the prince's kiss breaks an evil spell and makes everything right again. But in real life, giving mouth to mouth can't take away a sickness. Even if your father had performed CPR on your mother, she would have still had cancer, and she would have still died from it. There was nothing your father could do to take the sickness away."

Heather glowered at Katie in the semidarkness. "You're wrong."

"No, honey, I'm not wrong. Sometimes CPR can make a heart start beating again, but that's all it can do. It can't cure cancer."

Heather regarded her wordlessly, her deep blue eyes blazing into Katie's.

Katie reached out to hold Heather closer, but the little girl moved away. She crawled over to her sleeping bag and sat upright, still staring at Katie, her doll across her chest as if it were a shield.

"I still say he could've saved her," said Heather stubbornly. "I won't listen to you. You're lying. You're just like him. I don't believe you!"

"Heather, it was just a mistake. Nobody ever explained it to you before. It doesn't matter anymore, and now that you know the truth, you can stop hating your father—"

"I'll always hate him!"

The coldness and vehemence of her voice startled Katie. She tried to think of another way to explain the truth, but the angry, hostile look on Heather's face stopped her. Katie realized all at once what a heavy burden the child was now carrying; first, her guilt over running down the battery of the ELT, and now, realizing that she had been hating her father for something that wasn't his fault. No wonder Heather was resisting the truth. It must hurt terribly.

"Heather . . ."

"Go away! You're just like him! Get away from me!"

Katie felt inadequate to help Heather, unable to minister to the terrible hurt that was encompassing her little heart. She knew she needed to seek the Lord and ask for wisdom and insight to help this little girl, and the longer she remained in the tent, the more urgent the need became.

"We can talk later, Heather," said Katie. "You think about it for a little while, but try not to be so hard on yourself. You didn't know about the truth, and you're not to blame for making a mistake about your father."

"Go away!"

Katie smiled at her, trying to throw into that smile some sign that she understood and wanted to help her, but Heather turned away from her and cradled her doll in her arms, refusing to listen.

The fresh air outside the musty tent felt wonderful, as if it were blowing dust and cobwebs out of Katie's heart. She felt her spirits rising. At least she knew why she was here, stranded out in the middle of nowhere with this troubled family. No one else had recognized Heather's confusion. No one else had shown her the truth. Most of all, Katie's heart felt the release of the burden of suspicion she had carried against Mark since the first time Heather had accused him of killing her mother.

Mark was the victim of a terrible mistake. There was nothing he had done that he couldn't be forgiven for. Nothing that he couldn't be loved in spite of.

Mark looked up when Katie approached the fire, his tanned face showing his concern. "Is she all right?"

"She will be," said Katie. "She needs a little time to get used to the idea that she's the reason we're still out here."

"I didn't help much, the way I yelled at her." He was holding a thick stick in his hands and was cutting it in the feathering pattern that would make it an effective torch. He cut at it viciously, betraying the anger he felt against himself. "I brought her out here to get closer to her, then I screamed at her and made her feel guilty."

"Please don't blame yourself," said Katie. "She has to face it and deal with it. I think it might help."

"Oh, you do?" Mark's voice took on a sneering tone. "Now you're a psychiatrist, too? It isn't enough that you're preaching to one of my kids, now you're psychoanalyzing the other one!"

For the first time, Katie noticed that Laurie was sitting cross-legged by the fire with Katie's Bible open on her lap.

Laurie rushed to help. "I asked Katie questions, Dad. She didn't preach to me. She just answered—"

"If you want answers, you come to me. You don't need that malarkey. No one does." He turned his glare on Katie and she felt the heat of his anger shoot through her body. "I thought I told you to lay off my kids, Reed. They've got enough to work out without you complicating things with all your naive religious talk!"

Katie felt stabbed. She tried to muster up her dignity and not let her hurt show through. "I don't agree with you that 'religious talk' is naive, Mr. McLaren. Your two daughters are starving for the love and comfort of their heavenly Father . . ."

"They won't even take it from their real father, Reed! What makes you think you've got anything to offer them?"

"It's not me, Mr. McLaren. It's the Lord."

Mark sliced through the stick. He glared at it for a moment, then picked up the two pieces and pitched them into the campfire. "Just leave us alone, Reed," he said darkly. He reached over and yanked the Bible out of Laurie's hands. He flipped it closed and extended it to Katie. "And kindly keep this to yourself."

Katie received the Bible into her arms and held it the same way Heather had held her princess doll, as if it were a shield to protect her against the sting of unwanted truth. She felt herself moving quickly away from the fire, her heart thudding and her body suddenly shivering in the cold air. She had left the sweatshirt inside the tent with Heather.

She blinked back the pain of the tears that threatened to spill out of her eyes. Mark had sounded just like Steve, derisively rejecting the very foundation of her life and rejecting her along with it. The pain of her broken engagement rolled back over her and she lost her battle with the tears. They tracked cold paths down her cheeks and she quickly rubbed them away. For a moment the Bible weighed heavy in her arms, a dead weight that pulled her away from everything she wanted. She couldn't have Steve's love because of God. She couldn't have Mark's love, because of God. She couldn't—

Be unequally yoked.

She could almost hear Mary Grace's rebuke from one of their last talks.

"Forgive me," said Katie softly, eyes uplifted. "I've been so wrapped up in myself I haven't listened to you. You don't have accidents. You sent me here for a reason. I'm here to help these two precious girls and instead I'm acting like a schoolgirl over their father. I want to carry out my responsibilities, whatever they are. Please show me how to make your love and truth come real for them, Lord. Please show me the right way to minister to their needs. And . . ." Katie felt her own resistance to the prayer she was determined to pray. "Take away all the wrong feelings I have for Mark. I give them all up. I only want to have the feelings that you want me to have. The rest of my life isn't the issue here.

These people need something, and you've sent me here to deliver it. Show me how, please!"

The cold air pressed against her. She hugged her Bible to her chest and ducked her head against the wind. In the distance she heard the mountain lion screech. She heard Mark's voice coming from behind her.

He was standing by the girls' tent. While Katie watched, he knelt and spoke directly into the zippered flap. She thought she heard him say he was sorry. He stood up again and turned to his older daughter, and she obeyed a command Katie couldn't hear and went inside the tent to speak to her sister.

Mark saw Katie and turned his eyes away quickly. The movement didn't bother her. *He's got a lot on his heart,* she thought, *let him take one apology at a time.*

Laurie scrambled out of the tent, holding a silver whistle in her hand.

"What?" cried Mark. "What do you mean, she's gone?"

Nature was cruel. She waited until Mark, Laurie, and Katie realized Heather was missing, then viciously brought on the night. Darkness fell more quickly than it ever had before, blotting out the last feeble light of the day. Clouds spread out in front of the moon and stars, blocking their light and refusing to let even a tiny beam shine through to help. It was the darkest night Katie had ever experienced.

She was shivering violently. The sweatshirt was no help keeping away the daggering cold of the night wind. Her feet were tingling in the cold, making it even harder for her to keep her balance and step carefully over the dark ground. Only her face was warm, because of the heat blazing from the torch she held aloft in her right hand.

Mark was ahead of her, struggling with the uneven, dewy ground and the weight of both torch and rifle. He was straining to make out any sign that Heather had come this way, and still keep watch for predators. Laurie brought up the rear, stumbling over the rough terrain and calling her sister's name in a thin, frightened voice that vibrated in the sharp mountain air. The temperature had dropped alarmingly fast in the last hour. Katie clutched Heather's down ski jacket in her left hand and remembered all the times she had forgotten to take her own coat when she was a child. Heather could not have been thinking, could not have realized how terribly cold it was in the mountains at night . . . but her father knew, and it was plainly evident how terrified he was.

They had made no blaze marks in their haste to find the missing child. Katie wondered how they would ever find their way back to camp. Trekking over rough ground at night went against every rule of wilderness safety there was. Mark had to be desperate to take chances like this.

He was desperate. Caught between his need to find Heather and his need to keep Laurie and Katie safe, he had debated too quickly to make sense. He couldn't leave them alone in camp without the gun, but he couldn't take off alone at night without it. It was too dangerous to try to bring them along with him, risking the accidents and injuries that could make their situation far more deadly than it already was, but he couldn't wait until morning because his little girl didn't even have her coat and she wouldn't make it until morning. Even now, his voice cracking with fear and exertion, he called out for Heather and wished he could call out to someone to help them all. He wished there was someone somewhere who could hear him plead for Laurie and Katie's protection, beg safety for his younger daughter, beg that the impossible would happen and he would find her before the bear or the mountain lion did.

He wished there was someone to pray to. But he knew better.

Katie didn't. Laurie didn't. When their voices weren't calling out Heather's name they were jabbering all kinds of petitions to that empty sky that held no God.

"Heather!" he shouted. "Heather, where are you?"

The mountain lion screeched. It was somewhere close. Mark tightened his grip on the rifle. He should have tracked the lion and shot it. He should have tracked the bear and killed it. He should have eliminated the threats so that Heather wouldn't be in such terrible danger when she took it into her head to run away at dusk in the middle of a cold, dangerous wilderness.

He should have left her and her sister with their grandmother, where they were safe.

He should have refused to carry a passenger.

He should have torn that plane apart and inspected every nut and bolt before he put his family aboard it.

Mark shook with anguish and terror.

"Heather! Heather, where are you?" he shouted.

"Where is she? She is lost to our eyes, but not to yours. Show us where to look . . . your Word says light and dark are both alike to you . . . you can see her right now . . . guide us in the right direction. . . ."

Katie Reed. That crazy broad was turning his life upside down.

The mountain lion screeched.

"Over there!" shouted Katie. "I heard something!"

"It was the cougar!" shouted back Mark.

"No! Beyond the cougar. I hear crying! That way!" Katie pointed with the hand that held Heather's coat.

Mark turned immediately in that direction. He couldn't hear anything except the pounding of his own heart and the relentless whine of the wind. His torch cast eerie yellow shadows over the black earth. He strained to see farther through the blackness, thrusting his torch as far as he could to throw the light out in front of him.

Something flashed to his right. Mark wheeled, raising the burning light, trying to find it again. There! A flash, two flashes. The light of his fire reflected off something.

Eyes.

Yellow eyes with pinprick pupils.

"Mark! Look out!" cried Katie.

The cougar bared its teeth and crouched. One thick paw shot out, claws extended, batting the air in front of Mark in warning. Mark could not raise the rifle because of the torch. He waved the fire threateningly, and the big cat cringed and retreated a few yards. He advanced recklessly, and his light fell upon the dark maze of fir tree trunks behind the animal. The firelight gleamed off Heather's blond hair and illumined the shining path of the tears on her terrified face.

"There she is!" cried Laurie. "Heather!"

Mark cried out incoherently and leaped toward the cougar. It jumped aside, avoiding the flame, then screeched and batted its massive paw again. The claws caught Mark's jeans above the knee. Katie heard the fabric rip and saw a tinge of bright red spread down his thigh. She dropped Heather's coat and grabbed the torch with both hands, and charged.

The cougar twisted wildly, attacked on two sides by fire. Its growls rose above the noise of the wind as it jerked around, trying to fight and trying to escape. Katie caught the smell of burning fur and heard the beast scream. It writhed away from Mark's torch and skulked in a full circle around Katie. Mark was suddenly beside her, and the blaze from their combined torches lit up a swath of golden ground in front of the lion. The light blazed in its eyes and glinted against its long teeth and reddish gums. The big cat retreated, paused, circled in confusion and then bolted out of the light.

Mark and Katie moved in a slow circle, peering through the darkness, searching for the cat. It was gone.

"Where is she?" asked Mark. He had lost his bearings, couldn't see Heather anymore.

"Over there. With Laurie." Katie gestured with the torch. In the yellow wash of light they could see Laurie zipping her little sister into her ski jacket and pulling the hood up. Mark thudded across the ground toward them.

Heather was so small, scrunched up into a little ball with her face half-hidden by the hood of her jacket. Laurie stood up without a word and took the torch from her father. Katie came up behind him and automatically reached out for the rifle.

Mark held out his arms to his little girl.

"I don't want you!" she cried. But she lifted her arms to him anyway.

Katie didn't know how they found their way back to camp. The clouds had fled, exposing the earth to the radiant white light of the full moon. They came upon the stream almost at once, and Laurie extinguished one of the torches and used the other to light the ground in front of Mark's feet. He was limping slightly, and two broad streaks of blood had seeped down his leg to the hem of his jeans. They followed the stream for an hour at least, plodding along in exhaustion until the stream at last opened into the wide area where they fished. The moonlight bathed the scene in white light, showing clearly the blaze marks that guided them back to the empty tents and the campfire that had become their wilderness home.

Heather was sleeping soundly, her head bobbing up and down on Mark's shoulder. She didn't wake up when he set her down outside the tent, and she crawled in her sleep to the softness of her bag. Laurie climbed in behind her and unzipped Heather's jacket, easing it off and bringing the blankets up around her.

"I'll stay with her," she said.

Mark extinguished one torch and used the other one to set the campfire burning. Katie felt exhaustion fall over her, so much that she couldn't manage the few more yards to get to the tent. She sank down by the fire, yearning for her sleeping bag and for sleep. She knew if she rested for just a minute, she could make it the rest of the way.

"Katie?"

"Yes, Mark?"

"Thank you."

"You're welcome."

"Every time I cut loose on you, you end up doing something wonderful for my kids."

Katie shook her head. "It wasn't wonderful. It was necessary."

"I'm sorry."

"It's all right."

"No, it isn't. I'm sorry for all those things I said earlier. I've got no right to take all this out on you."

133

His apology was so sincerely spoken that Katie felt warmed, even more so than by the fire.

"Don't worry about it, please."

"I shouldn't have brought you all out here. It was a stupid idea to begin with. I wasn't there when they needed me, and there's no way a camping trip could restore the year the locust devoured."

Another biblical reference. Katie wondered how he knew so many.

"Maybe it will do more good than you think," she said.

"It's just going to make it harder to lose them again."

"Maybe you won't."

"Their grandmother is suing for permanent custody. They want to go on living with her. When we get back, it's all over."

"They may change their minds."

"No, they won't. They'll listen to anybody but me. That's why I got so worked up when I saw Laurie with your Bible . . . that, and a bunch of bad memories."

"About your wife?"

Mark nodded. "When I saw that Bible, all I could think about was that last, terrible year."

Katie thought about Steve, about Mary Grace, about being unequally yoked.

"It's very hard for non-Christians to live with Christians," she said quietly. "Believe me, I understand."

"So do I. The preaching can drive you crazy. When I got wound up, Adrian would leave the room and lock herself in her studio."

Katie's eyes slid over to him. "You?"

"Hard to imagine, isn't it?"

Katie sat up, her tiredness suddenly gone. "You? You were a Christian? I thought it was Adrian!"

"I don't remember what she was that year. She was a Buddhist for a while, but that was before TM. She was always into reincarnation. She got around to being almost everything, except a Christian. She never tried that. I guess she didn't have the same need I had."

"You?" Katie still couldn't grasp it.

"That was the year I was working out of a firehouse on the edge of the slums. I saw more gunshot wounds and stabbings . . . there were people so battered you couldn't tell if they were men or women, and some of them were out of their minds on drugs. I kept getting more and more depressed. One night was so bad I just started hollering that I couldn't take it anymore. The ambulance driver took me aside and started witnessing. I was starving. I ate it up. I got on my knees right there outside the emergency room."

Katie watched the firelight flicker over his tanned, tired face. She sensed that he needed to talk it out.

"What happened, Mark?"

"The usual stuff. I felt like it was real. Every night I wasn't working I was at a meeting somewhere. I started taking the girls to Sunday school. Adrian hated that. She thought I should wait until they grew up and let them decide for themselves. Then I went to work on her. We'd never had a good marriage, and we would've quit it if it weren't for Heather. We decided to stick it out for her sake and I suppose we did all right until that year. She couldn't take life with a Jesus freak. I preached her right into another man's arms."

"Oh, Mark."

"Don't tell Laurie."

"Of course I won't."

"She adored Adrian. I don't want her to know that."

"I won't tell her."

"I didn't know about it for a long time. I kept right on preaching. I was going to see her born again if it killed me. But it didn't kill me. It killed her."

"What?"

Mark leaned back against the rocks and stretched his legs out toward the fire. Katie saw the bloodstain on his leg and felt a twinge of alarm. He saw her expression and shook his head. "It isn't that bad. I'll take care of it later. I used to do it for a living."

"What do you mean, 'it killed her'?"

"Adrian knew something was wrong with her. She thought she had—you know, V.D. She was afraid to tell me, so she kept putting it off. It's funny how people will do that. Even when they suspect they might be seriously ill, they'll deny it and hide from it and never do anything about it until it's too late. Adrian was like that.

"She finally told me. I was shocked. I couldn't believe it—Adrian, having an affair. I knew I was supposed to forgive her and I tried to, but I felt so betrayed. Then we went to the doctor and found out it wasn't V.D. It was something else."

"Cancer."

"She let it go too long. It spread. There wasn't anything they could do, except try chemotherapy. She refused. I couldn't blame her. I've seen what it can do to people."

"I'm so sorry."

"I begged her to accept the Lord. I pleaded with her to get saved. Then one night she asked me to get out. She said she could take the pain and sickness better than she could take me. I drove out to the mountains and spent the whole night praying for her to be healed. Adrian died while I was gone. The girls were there alone with her. Laurie was holding her hand." Mark rubbed his hand over his eyes. "That same ambulance driver who witnessed to me took the call. He told me later how hysterical Heather was, and how hard Laurie cried. . . ."

Katie wasn't aware that she had moved until Mark rested his head against her shoulder. She put her arms around him and felt his winding around her. She rested her cheek against his hair and felt herself engulfed in the enormity of his pain and regret.

"And you blamed God, didn't you?"

"There's no God to blame."

"You know there is. You knew him once."

"It's all lies, Katie. I heard what I wanted to hear and I held on to it past the time I should've known better. I don't believe in God anymore. I can't."

"You can't?"

"Don't you see, Katie? I have to believe it was all a lie. It's either that he's not up there, or else he is and just doesn't care."

136

Katie closed her eyes. She kissed his hair. "Oh, Mark. He does care. I don't know why Adrian died, but God is there and he does care. . . ."

"Daddy?"

Mark jerked around. Katie released him at once. Laurie had come out of the tent and was standing behind them. Katie could see the terrible strain on her young face.

"I'll, uh, I'll go stay with Heather," said Katie lamely. She stood up quickly and started toward the tent, but she had only gone a few feet when she heard Laurie say, "Is it true? What you said about Mom and another . . . ?"

Katie knelt by the flap. She slid off her shoes and began to back into the tent, then saw Mark and Laurie silhouetted against the firelight, rocking in each other's arms. She heard snatches of words, of sobs, coming from them both. Their breakthrough had finally come.

"Thank you, Lord," she whispered, and as she did she felt peace descend over her, that warm sense of well-being that assured her that there was a purpose for this time and this whole situation, and that some of it had already been fulfilled. Katie focused on Mark and Laurie again and felt her heart filling with love for them both. She nestled into her sleeping bag, and impulsively reached over to touch Heather. Before Katie fell asleep, she breathed a prayer that Heather, too, would be reconciled to her father, and love him again.

CHAPTER 12

FROST COVERED THE GROUND the next morning. Katie's leather loafers slipped and slid on the slick, wet surface as she struggled from the woodpile to the campfire. Overhead a flock of noisy geese honked and flapped, flying in a perfect V-formation, heading south.

Winter was coming. She could smell it in the air. Katie automatically glanced up at the peaks of the mountains and saw that the snow had grown heavier. There was no fear in her heart this time; even though the weather was turning bitter she knew they were in no danger. The Lord had been hard at work in their little camp. Soon it would be time to leave.

Katie squinted at the sky and wondered if rescue would come today.

Heather tottered out of the tent, her hair tousled. She noticed the frost and her eyes opened wide. "Snow!"

"It's only frost, Heather. But that's almost snow." Katie pulled her hood up over her head and pulled the drawstrings until the hood fit snugly. Heather rubbed her eyes sleepily and followed her to the fire. Katie fed the fire a few twigs and breathed in its warmth as it crackled to life. Heather leaned against her, and Katie slid her arm around her and hugged her close.

"Is Laurie still asleep?"

"Laurie's already up."

"Where did she go?" Katie looked around. In the distance she saw the tail of the *Adrian* moving jerkily.

Heather saw it too. "The plane's moving!"

Katie dropped the rest of the wood into the fire and headed toward Mark's tent. "Mark! Something's happening to the plane!" There was no answer, and Katie hesitated outside the tent, feeling too shy to bend and look inside. She wished there were a doorbell she could ring.

Mark wasn't in the tent. Belatedly she saw the imprint of his boots in the frost. The tail of the *Adrian* moved again, and she held out her hand to Heather. "Let's go see what's up."

Heather obediently took her hand and walked along beside her. Katie felt a surge of affection for the little girl, and squeezed her hand impulsively. Heather smiled and squeezed back, then her little, heart-shaped face suddenly mirrored confusion. "What are they doing?"

Mark and Laurie were working on the airplane. At first Katie thought they were trying to repair it, then realized that Mark was pulling off the tires. Laurie was in the cabin, using his Buck knife to cut through the blue upholstery and pull the stuffing out of the seats.

"Good morning," called Mark. "You're probably wondering why we're trashing the airplane."

"It crossed my mind."

"We're going to take all this stuff over by the signal fire. The next time a plane comes along, we'll be able to throw on the tires and get a heavy, black column of smoke. There's no way a plane could miss seeing that."

"Is it going to come back?" asked Heather in a small voice.

"Any time now," said Katie.

"It better come back soon," Mark said. "We're almost out of coffee."

"But not cookies." Laurie pulled out two foil-wrapped bags of gingersnaps from the hold. "I think Dad brought enough to last the whole winter!"

139

Katie laughed along with her, her heart soaring. The shyness she had felt a while ago was gone. Mark was in a good mood, and the change in his relationship with Laurie was obvious. She watched with growing elation as Mark put his arms up and swung Laurie off the wing of the plane, putting her down after a quick hug.

Breakfast was festive. Mark used some of the carefully rationed supplies and made sourdough flapjacks. The aroma of warm maple syrup reminded Katie of the first morning she had awakened here, and she wondered whether this would be the last. Mark flipped the pancakes expertly, trading jokes with Laurie and spinning tall tales about his early days as a guide and bush pilot. Heather didn't respond, but she listened.

The day brought no rescue planes.

During the afternoon the temperature plummeted. Mark's good mood began to slip. He studied the heavy snow on the peaks and scanned the sky for airplanes.

"Maybe tomorrow," he said uncertainly.

Laurie hugged his arm. "I hope not. It's just starting to get fun."

By the eighteenth day, Katie was wearing two of Mark's T-shirts under her sweater. The fish stopped biting, and Mark turned more and more to the dwindling store of supplies to feed them.

"When will it start snowing?" Katie asked him.

"Not until after we've gone, I hope."

"It doesn't look good, does it?"

"Do you want the truth?"

"Yes."

"What are we going to do?"

"Wait."

"You still don't think we could try walking out?"

"We may have to, if we aren't found soon."

"How long can we wait?"

"Not much longer."

Katie was no longer afraid, but as the days dragged by she shivered in her inadequate clothing and began to ask God what was taking so long. Mark and Laurie had reconciled; the girl followed her father everywhere,

140

chattering as if to make up for the year they had lost. Heather still wouldn't speak to him, but she had stopped complaining and watched him intently. Was there more work to be done with Heather before the Lord would bring them home? Or was it Mark's disillusioned, backslidden heart that was on the line?

Katie didn't know. She only prayed.

They had been lost in the Montana Rockies three weeks when Katie realized that she had begun to love Mark's daughters. It had happened so gradually she hadn't noticed. Katie brushed and braided Heather's hair and helped Laurie wash their clothes in the stream, feeling as if they were now all part of the same family. She zipped Heather's jacket up and reminded Laurie to put on her mittens. At night she tucked Heather in and read Bible stories aloud. Heather listened to them as if they were fairy tales, but Laurie listened for the meanings and asked questions. Katie was amazed at the depth of her hunger to learn the Word, and wished Laurie's father could experience the same thing.

Just as Katie realized she loved the girls, she also came to know that every day she felt relieved when rescue did not come. She felt a growing sadness in her heart, knowing that rescue would cut her off from Laurie and Heather. She ached at the thought of losing touch with them.

And with Mark.

Something had changed between them since the night Heather ran away.

His caustic remarks had stopped. He never called her "Reed" anymore. More and more he opened up to her, talking about his boyhood adventures and his years as pilot, paramedic, and flight instructor. Katie listened, fascinated, and told him about her own life. She described Mary Grace Kimball and their close, loving friendship. She even told him about the year of her life she had spent with Steve.

"It's a good thing it fell through," was his only comment.

He hadn't tried to touch her again. She had suddenly

been elevated to the status of friend. Katie was pleased by the intimacy she shared with him, but she was also troubled. Knowing about Mark's past with the Lord had excited her. She had felt for the first time that she was not becoming unequally yoked, and that Mark's heart could be turned back to God. She had let her fantasies run away with her, imagining that there could be a future for her in his family. But Mark's friendly behavior stopped at that. He kept his distance and spoke to her as if she were his sister, and Katie struggled with disappointment.

She watched the sky and dreaded the day the plane would come back. Mark would probably clap her on the shoulder and smile before he thanked her for her help and walked out of her life for good.

"What will you do when you get home?" she asked him one night.

Mark stared into the campfire, his expression suddenly serious.

"It depends on the girls. If they go back to live with their grandmother, I'll probably keep flying. There won't be anything to go home to. If I get to keep Laurie, I'll go back to the emergency squad so I can make a home for her . . . but that probably won't happen. Their grandmother already had a lawyer when we left."

"Has Laurie said anything about where she wants to live?"

"Yes. With me." Mark's voice caught. "I never thought she'd even speak to me again, and now she wants to come home with me. It's a downright miracle."

Katie smiled. "That's exactly what it is."

"Not that kind." He shook his head. "I didn't mean to imply that God had anything to do with it."

"How do you know?"

"It doesn't make sense. If there was a God, why would he just now start to get interested? Where was he when I needed him?" Mark snapped a twig in two and threw the pieces into the fire. "If there was a God behind all this, wouldn't things be better with Heather, too? No, it's just a coincidence that Laurie came around. Heather still wishes I'd drop dead."

"Things are better with Heather," said Katie. She told him about the little girl's confusion, and how she had mixed up a fairy tale kiss with mouth-to-mouth resuscitation.

Mark listened, amazed.

"So that's it!" he exclaimed. "I would have never figured that out! It's a lucky thing you came along on this trip."

"Luck had nothing to do with it, Mark. God revealed Heather's problem to me."

"Don't sell yourself short. You figured it out by yourself."

Katie shook her head. "No, Mark. It was God."

"Okay. I'm sure you believe that, and that's fine. After all you've done for us, I'd be a real jerk to argue with you about it. I don't happen to believe it, but you do, so . . . fine."

"You can't believe there's a purpose to all this?"

"No."

"Maybe the engine failed and stranded you here so God could show you the way back to your daughters?"

"Coincidence."

Katie reached over and touched his sleeve. "You've already won Laurie's love again. Now you understand what's coming between you and Heather. You wouldn't have any of that if you'd just camped out for a week and taken them back home. Don't you see, there's a reason?"

"Lucky breaks."

"Mark."

He stood up and turned away from her. "I'm sorry. I can't accept that. If I did, I'd have to accept the idea that there's a God at all, and that he cares, and I've had enough experience to prove that's a crock."

They ran out of food the next day.

"That should prove something to you," said Mark darkly. "If there was a God watching over us, shouldn't we have a miracle catch? Shouldn't there be pigeons from the desert, or manna on the ground?"

He spent the evening cleaning his rifle. "I've got to go

hunting. I don't know how we're going to find anything with four of us thrashing around making noise, but we'll all have to go. I can't leave you here without the gun."

"You have to leave us," said Katie. "We have to stay near the signal fire. What if a plane comes over while we're gone?"

Mark hesitated.

"We'll be all right," prodded Katie.

"What about the bear?"

"What bear? We haven't seen that bear in weeks. He disappeared the same time the mountain lion did. Don't worry about us. Whether or not you believe it, the Lord is standing watch over this camp. We'll be safe." She crossed her arms, immovable.

Mark thought it over, his eyes flicking from the gun to the pyramid of wood that would signal their need for help.

"I don't like this," he said. "I don't like this at all."

"So what else is new?" said Katie. "Go hunting. We're in good hands."

Katie was up before dawn, but Mark was already up, laying a fire. She listened to his last minute instructions, although she knew all the rules by now.

"Build the fire up high and keep it that way. Most animals won't come near fire. If any do . . ."

"They won't." Katie removed the silver chain from around her neck and dropped it over Mark's head. The whistle gleamed in the early morning light. "Remember, three blasts is the signal for help."

"Did I create this monster?" Mark rolled his eyes and emptied a box of shells into his vest pocket.

Katie felt his breath warm her cheek as he leaned toward her to kiss her, but he pulled back abruptly and he clapped her on the shoulder instead.

"I'll be home for dinner," he promised. "I have to, since I'm bringing it."

He picked up his rifle and started off.

Katie waved and he responded. She hoped he was too far away to see the tears that slipped down her cheeks.

Dawn and dusk were the best times for hunting deer. Those were the times they left their bedding areas to feed. Mark walked steadily in the direction of the stream, heading for the place where he had found the cougar's kill. There was a stand of pines nearby. It was a good place to start looking.

It wasn't long before Mark found what he was looking for. He saw worn areas across the trunk of a small tree, and his search of nearby trees turned up more. Mark recognized them as rubs, places where young bucks scraped their new antlers to rid them of the blood vessels clinging to them, curiously called velvet. Mark found five rubs within a short distance. There must be a buck somewhere close with a very polished rack on his head.

Mark looked around for a suitable tree and climbed until he was about twelve feet above the ground. It would be easier to sight deer from this vantage point, and it would help to conceal him. Mark nestled between two branches and waited.

Waiting was the hard part.

Mark's stomach rumbled, reminding him that his family was counting on him. He was sweating slightly, although the morning air was briskly cold. This was the situation Mark had dreaded most—being responsible for their survival.

From the moment the plane had taken off, they had all looked to him to know what to do. They had obeyed his instructions to prepare for their forced landing, and expected him to lead them through the days following. It had been up to him to set up camp and blaze trail markers. It was the gun in his hands that had watched over their fishing expeditions and their sleep. It was up to him to build the signal pyre. It had been his decision to light torches and go searching for Heather, and his decision which direction to take.

Now he had to provide for them.

Why did everyone assume it was the man's job to do that?

Mark knew he was better equipped than most men to do the job. He had years of experience, beginning from

145

the time he was a boy. He had been given his first gun at eight, and bagged his first deer on the second day of the season. Years of bush piloting, working as a guide for anxious deer hunters, had sharpened his skills. He knew how to find deer, how to shoot them, how to field-dress and cook them.

Provided they showed up.

Mark relaxed in the tree and let his thoughts wander. It was the first time he had been alone since the landing. Even at night he was preoccupied with the others, sleeping lightly, always listening for the noise of an intruding animal in the camp.

Although Katie Reed was a match for any of them.

Mark thought of her banging the flashlight on the wolverine and smiled to himself. She had been ready to swing at the bear, too, and she had charged the mountain lion. She was something else.

Mark curled his lip and thought about it.

She was more than he had first realized. In three weeks his reaction to her had changed completely. At first she had been a nuisance, a Glory Mountain candidate with a Bible under her arm. Then she had been a help, looking after the girls, defending them, catching fish and even cleaning them. She had swallowed her distaste a dozen times to rise to the need of the moment. He liked that.

He had used it, too. More than once when the heaviness of his responsibility began to weigh him down, he turned to the only warm woman within reach for comfort.

But she was more than convenient now.

Mark had told her things he had never told anyone else. He liked to make her laugh. He liked to tease her until she grinned and began to tease back. He liked to watch her moving around the camp, bulky in her many layers of clothing, most of it his. He liked the way she had befriended his girls, and he liked the difference she had made in Laurie.

He liked the way she had held him when the pain of Adrian had wracked him, the night Heather ran away.

Mark sighed. He knew himself well enough to know

that he didn't act impulsively. He thought out every step, planned carefully, never let his heart take advantage of his head.

Until now.

He was falling in love with Katie Reed, and he didn't want to.

He didn't want to love a Christian.

That was the only thing about her he couldn't accept. There was a power to her, an underlying confidence in the justice of a God he had proven unjust. She believed sincerely in the love of a God he knew to be unloving. She lived her life by the Word, a Word he had found to be absolutely untrue.

She reminded him of someone else, of a man who had grasped the gospel of Jesus Christ and lived by it steadfastly until the night it had all come crashing down. Someday it would crash down on Katie Reed, and he didn't want to be around when it did.

He heard the swish of the pine boughs and looked up sharply.

The buck was big, bigger than he had expected. It walked with fluid grace, the early morning sun gleaming off its soft brown coat. Mark paused, marvelling at the sheer majesty of the animal. It was stunning, its graceful head held aloft, crowned with an immense rack of sharp-edged, polished antlers.

Mark raised the rifle and sighted.

The deer moved slowly, taking its time. It was turned slightly away from him, concealing its vulnerable heart. Mark heard it snorting softly. It stopped, delicately sniffing the air.

Mark was facing into the wind to conceal his scent. For a moment he flashed back to the last flight of the *Adrian*, and the vital need to keep the plane facing into the wind to keep it aloft. He recalled the landing, his unaccustomed fear and the terrible, deadening shock he had felt afterward. He remembered fighting it all down to provide for the needs of his girls.

He had to provide for them now. He moved slightly, adjusting the rifle and kept his bead on the deer.

The buck stayed still, waiting. It turned toward him. The heart was almost clear.

One more step, Mark said to himself. *Just one more.*

The animal stood poised regally, surveying the woods. It stared in Mark's direction for a moment, but there was no reaction, no sudden flight. It hadn't seen him. It didn't know he was there.

The deer stepped forward.

Mark fired. The buck jerked violently. It took off at a run. Mark leaped from the tree, the jar of the impact spiraling through his legs up to his knees. The leg with the cougar claw gash ached with the jolt.

The buck ran true for about thirty yards, then staggered. It sank to the damp, loamy earth. It struggled erect, but only managed a few more yards. It dropped clumsily and lay still on the ground.

Mark felt a wild stab of excitement. He had done it. He had provided. Katie Reed would say the Lord had provided, but Mark knew better. He knew the movement of the deer was determined by nature, not by God. Mark had brought it down, not God. Mark had provided. Not God.

Mark limped forward, admiring the rack of antlers. He regretted that this wasn't a leisurely sportsman's hunt, with the benefit of taking the deer head to mount as a trophy. Pity. It was a beautiful animal. It was incredibly large and powerful looking, even as it lay with its back toward him in the early morning light.

Mark circled it slowly, admiring. Then he saw that the eyes were closed. They should have been open. He searched quickly for the tongue, which should have flopped out of the deer's mouth. It wasn't there. Mark backed off a step. The buck shuddered, and abruptly bolted to its feet and charged.

Mark gasped when two hundred pounds of desperate animal plowed into him, knocking the wind out of his lungs and sending his rifle flying from his hand. His back slammed against the hard earth, and he rolled sideways to escape those sharp, polished antlers. The weight of the buck came down across the back of his legs and he kicked frantically, trying to push it away. He rolled over onto his back and fought to sit up, but it was too late.

The buck dropped its head and thrust against him. He felt the sharp point of the antler spear his leg and blood spurted up around it. The pain caught him up short and he heard himself cry out.

The buck pushed against him with diminishing strength, then feebly withdrew. It staggered sideways, fell over its own feet and hit the ground with a dull thud. This time the eyes were open. The tongue lolled out of the side of its mouth. Mark had made his kill.

He tore off his sock cap and shoved it against the gaping hole in his leg. He concentrated, forcing all his strength into the heels of his hands, trying to apply enough pressure to stop the rush of blood. A wave of nausea washed over him. His grip slackened and he fought to stay conscious, to keep staunching the flow of blood before he blacked out and bled to death.

It was soaking through the knit fibers of his hat. He pressed harder. He was leaning into it with all his strength, groaning with the pain and hearing his own voice forming words: "Don't do it! Don't do it! They need me!"

He wasn't sure whether he was pleading with himself, or nature, or the God he no longer believed in.

He let go of the hat with one hand, long enough to fish for the whistle Katie had placed around his neck. He pulled it out from his sweater and felt his own warmth as he pressed his lips around it. Dizziness overwhelmed him, and he knew he didn't have the strength to force air through it. It didn't matter anyway. He was too far from the camp to be heard.

He was losing consciousness. He fought off the descending blackness. The whistle became cold in his mouth. He summoned up every particle of strength in his body and blew. The shrillness of the blasts vibrated painfully in his ears. One, two, three—he gave the universal signal of distress. He felt faint and sick, and knew he didn't have the strength to blow it again. The whistle fell from his lips and dangled uselessly on its chain.

Mark's head was too heavy to hold up any longer. His cheek hit the cold ground. He was flooded with the scent of pine, of soil, of his own blood. He gritted his teeth against the pain in his leg and fought numbness overcoming every limb.

"Please . . . ," he groaned, "please don't . . . they'll die out here without me!"

The buzzing darkness fell.

CHAPTER 13

MARK WOKE SOMETIME AFTER NOON. He'd been lying for hours on the cold, hard ground, and when he shifted, sticks and stones poked his side and legs. The buck lay motionless in front of him, with Mark's own blood drying on its antlers.

The pain was terrible. Mark's whole leg throbbed. His body was stiff and ached all over, and his hands had become numb from pressing his gaping wound.

Every time he tried to move, the wound opened and bled again. He knew he would never make it back to camp.

The chain around his neck bit coldly into his skin. He rested, breathing deeply, until he managed the strength to lift the whistle to his lips again. It was a futile gesture, nevertheless, he summoned up his strength and sounded three more blasts.

Pain spiralled up his leg. He groaned and dropped the whistle. He felt himself sinking, losing control over the engulfing darkness. His head dropped back against the ground, and unconsciousness rolled over him.

The next time he opened his eyes, he saw Katie Reed. "Oh, thank God," she whispered. "Stay awake, Mark, please! You've got to tell me what to do!"

He didn't know what she was doing here. She was supposed to be back in the camp, watching for airplanes, watching over his children. It made no sense that she was here, and he knew he was hallucinating.

"Mark, please! What do I do?"

He pried open his eyes. "Pressure."

He felt Katie remove the bloodstained sock cap from his leg.

"It's not bleeding now," she said.

He had to force his words out. "Go back . . . get the first-aid box—"

"I've got it with me. Now what?"

"You've got it?"

"You told me that the first day we were here. You said if I ever heard three blasts on the whistle, grab the first-aid kit and go to help."

"Good girl, Katie."

His head swam. He heard the case snap open.

"Stay with me, Mark."

"Peroxide."

Katie pawed through the supplies. "Here it is."

"Pour it over," he commanded.

"Are you sure?"

He laughed feebly.

"Of course you're sure," she said lamely. "It's your job."

Mark heard the cap open. She hesitated, then reached for the sheath on his belt. She unsnapped it and drew out his Buck knife. He felt her cut away the fabric around the wound.

Katie cleaned out the wound with peroxide. He heard her gasp when she saw it.

"It's supposed to look like that," he said weakly.

She poured more peroxide. "It's fizzing."

"Supposed to."

"What now?"

"Pressure bandage. Tight . . . don't cut off my circ—"

"Like this?"

"Good. Good." Mark felt himself fading. He heard a slight snap, then suddenly his senses were engulfed in the pungent stench of ammonia. Coherence flooded back. He felt as if he were being lifted out of darkness.

"Dad?" It was Laurie. "Are you going to be all right?"

He nodded. The movement of his head made him dizzy.

"What happened to you, Daddy?"

He pointed at the antlers, then his leg. "The buck stops here."

"Oh, Daddy!"

"Cute, Mark," said Katie. "You're bleeding to death and cracking jokes about it."

"I'm not bleeding to death. Not now, anyway." He rested from the effort of talking for a moment. "How did you find me?"

"We followed the whistle, just like you told us to."

Mark knew he was losing coherence again. They couldn't have heard his whistle all the way back in the camp.

"That's impossible," he murmured.

"With God all things are possible," whispered Laurie to Katie.

Mark heard it, but he had no energy to protest. He felt Katie elevating his leg and it felt better. The throbbing became less intense. "Where'd you learn to do that?"

"Steve taught me," she answered, and noticed that Mark winced at the sound of the name. She told herself it was from pain, not from hearing the name of a man she had once cared for. "What's going to happen now? Should we try to make some kind of a litter and drag you back to camp? What do we do?"

"I'll manage. I'll walk."

"You and whose wheelchair?"

"I'm already feeling better. Give me some time."

"Are we talking about weeks or months?"

"Courage, Katie. I'm stronger than I look."

"I hope so, because you look like a limp dishrag to me." Katie waved the ammonia capsule under his nose. Consciousness rushed back, choking him.

"Enough! I'm woozy, but I'm not dead." He laid back

and thought he heard Heather's voice, far away, asking Katie if he was going to die. He was almost relieved when he heard Katie say he wasn't.

"What time is it?"

Katie pushed his sweater up above his watch. "It's almost two o'clock."

"It's after lunch time," said Heather from somewhere far away.

Mark's eyes flickered over the buck. "There it is, gang. Dig in."

"That's not funny!" snapped Heather.

"Give him a break, would you?" said Laurie crossly. "He almost got killed getting food for us. The least you can do is laugh at his jokes."

"I'm wounded—I'm not pathetic," whispered Mark. "Laurie, how much do you remember about field-dressing game?"

"What's that?" asked Katie.

"Cutting up the meat," Laurie answered.

"Close enough," said Mark. "It's doing it in a sanitary way."

"I don't think I remember much," said Laurie. She frowned at the deer, giving it a nudge with her foot. "I only watched you do it once."

Mark heaved, trying to breathe deeply enough to clear his head. "I'm going to have to talk you through it."

"Talk me through it?"

"Like pilots talk other pilots through landings," said Katie.

"Another cheap shot, Katie."

"I didn't mean it that way."

"I know." He groped for her hand, found it and squeezed it. "Are you ready for a new experience to tell your grandchildren?"

Katie nodded. "I just hope my grandchildren have strong stomachs."

"I'll do whatever you say, Daddy," said Laurie bravely.

Mark didn't know how they managed it. Katie built the fire they used to sterilize the knife, and Laurie did the cutting, moving slowly, afraid of making a mistake and spoiling the meat. Heather hung back, saying nothing but an occasional "Yuck." Katie helped Laurie handle the heavy buck, and they were soon lunching on roast venison.

The food restored Mark faster than the ammonia had. He felt alive for the first time since the buck had gored him. Katie covered the fire with dirt. She offered herself as a crutch for the trip back. Laurie and Heather carried as much of the meat as they could, although most of it was left behind for the predators.

They were a long way from camp when they heard the plane.

For two days Mark needed help getting in and out of his tent. He spent most of his time beside the fire with his leg elevated, watching Katie and his girls take care of all those things he thought only he could do. Katie managed to cut firewood without cutting herself, and kept the fire burning briskly. Laurie and Heather hauled water and washed dishes, burning the boughs and keeping the site clean. When the deer meat was gone, Laurie went fishing and came back with a string of smallmouth bass and lake trout. Katie watched over them all with Mark's rifle over her arm, and everytime she went by she left Mark a small stack of gingersnaps.

But he still couldn't understand how they had found him.

"We heard the whistle," said Katie.

"I was too far away."

"The sound must have carried on the thin mountain air."

"That's impossible. I was too far away. And how did you find me out there? I could have been anywhere in a five-mile radius. . . ."

"I told you. We followed the whistle."

"That's impossible. I only blew it twice."

Katie exchanged a look with Laurie. "Only twice?"

"What are you two looking so strange for?"

Laurie started to giggle. "You either blew it in your sleep, or else there's one heck of an echo out there!"

155

Mark dropped the subject.

The thin air and the cold tired the girls out quickly. They began going to bed right after dinner every night. Laurie usually read herself to sleep, and Katie would turn off the flashlight when she came into the tent later. Her father's survival had boosted Laurie's new found faith immeasurably, but Heather was depressed over missing the second plane. She retreated to her doll and a glum silence.

Mark was depressed, too.

When it was his time to relieve Katie, he took the rifle across his lap and raised his injured leg up on his pack. "Are you still convinced there's a God looking out for you?" he asked Katie before she left him. "I notice He didn't light the signal fire for us when we were too far away to do it ourselves."

Katie smiled. "Maybe he's not finished with us yet."

Mark shook his head. "I hope you're wrong. What else can happen?"

Katie's cheerfulness and steady faith bewildered Mark. He watched her covertly and was both fascinated and irritated. In the last month, Katie Reed had become the most infuriating and desirable woman he had ever known.

Mark fought with himself. He did not want to fall in love with a Christian.

By the evening of the thirty-first day, he knew he had.

Katie asked him again about walking out. "Do you think anyone could still be looking for us after a whole month?"

"They might be," he answered. "Even if they aren't we've spotted two planes, and any traffic in the area means hope. I still think our best chance of being found is to stay by the plane and the signal fire."

"How long can we wait? It's already October." Katie pointed to the thick snow on the peaks. Mark looked up and shook his head. "Let's give it a few more days. I need more time to heal before I start out on a hike that long."

It began to snow the next afternoon.

When Mark felt the moist coldness of the snowflakes touching his hands and face, he felt a stab of panic. He hadn't expected snow so soon.

At any time the fierce mountain winds could collide with sudden heavy snowfalls and trap them in a sea of deadly drifts. They had waited as long as they could. They had to get out now. Mark told Katie his decision to break camp after she had said good night to the girls.

"The snow didn't stick," she pointed out. "And it stopped after an hour. Maybe there won't be any more for a while."

"We can't gamble on that. As it is, we may get caught in the snow on our way out. We've got to get going."

"Can you make it?" She looked doubtfully at the leg he still favored.

"I'll have to. We'll take the blankets and sleeping bags. We'll have to leave your tent, but we'll take mine so the girls will have some shelter from the wind at night. We'll need the first-aid kit, of course, and the survival gear. Everything else has to stay."

"How long will it take us to get . . . somewhere?"

"There's no telling. We won't make good time with the girls and we'll have to cut it short every day in time to set up camp before dark. We can't get in a hurry because of the danger of injuries. We'll take it one careful step at a time."

"I don't think you answered my question."

"We could walk for a week. I won't lie to you, Katie. This is a dangerous thing we're planning to do. If I thought there was any chance we might be spotted and picked up before the weather gets worse, I'd want us to stay put. We're taking an awful chance by moving out."

"I'll stay as close to Heather as I can. She's the one who will need the most help."

"I appreciate that. Maybe I haven't told you, but I've noticed the way you've taken my girls under your wing. You're making a real difference in them."

"They're wonderful girls, Mark. I'm going to miss them when—" Katie broke off and poked at the fire with a stick.

157

"When we get home?"

"Yes."

"I'll miss them, too. If their grandmother was serious about that custody suit, she'll take them back the minute we hit town."

"Isn't Laurie almost old enough to choose?"

"She'll be fourteen in January. I don't know if she'll leave Heather, though. They had to lean on each other during the last year, when I was gone."

"Sooner or later, Heather is going to realize the truth. Someday she's going to understand that you weren't to blame for her mother's death, and when that happens, she'll come back to you."

"I hope so." Mark stared into the fire for a few minutes.

Katie didn't mind the silences that occasionally fell between them. Even when they weren't speaking, she had a sense of close companionship with him that felt comfortable and secure.

Mark cleared his throat. "What will you do when you get back?"

"Go back to the hospital and see if I still have a job."

"Do you think they would have replaced you this fast?"

"I hope not."

"You'll probably spend time with your friend Mary Grace, won't you?"

Katie nodded. "I've got lots of things to talk over with her."

"And will you see Steve, too?"

Katie hesitated, surprised. "No, I don't think so. There's no reason for me to see him now."

"You don't think he might have changed his mind about you by now? Your being lost out here might have scared him into some second thoughts."

"It doesn't matter what Steve thinks. I was the one who made the decision not to marry him, and nothing has happened to change that."

"I see."

"Even if he were to change his mind about . . . things, I don't think it would make any difference for us."

"What things? Your religion?"

"Yes."

"So if you went home and found out he had become a Christian, you still wouldn't want him back?"

Katie felt embarrassed and confused. She couldn't tell Mark what was really on her heart, that Steve couldn't compare to *him*. She felt a wave of sadness and discouragement wash over her, and she steeled herself against it. She had tried hard to accept the fact that she couldn't remain with Mark, but now that the time was coming when they would leave the wilds and go back home, she felt especially lonely. Mark had awakened a love in her she hadn't suspected she was capable of, and she knew it would be a long, long time before she would be able to open her heart to any other man. "No, I don't want him back."

Mark reached out tentatively and took her hand. Katie felt an electric thrill course through her.

"Katie . . ."

"You've been a pretty good friend, too," she said quickly. "I'm even going to miss you."

"You don't have to miss me." He squeezed her hand gently. "It's funny how things can happen when we don't really expect them to. I didn't plan this, Katie. I really didn't expect—"

"To be stranded in the mountains."

"To fall in love with you."

Katie's heart thumped so hard she felt faint. She had yearned for weeks to hear Mark say those very words. He had spoken them to her in a dozen different ways in a dozen different dreams, but now they were real. The love she had tried to squelch surged up and overflowed from her heart, and in spite of her effort to control them, tears of joy sparkled in her shining brown eyes.

Mark stood up and pulled her to her feet. He was gentle, his fingertips caressing her cheeks while he kissed her. The tears spilled out of her eyes and he kissed them away, breathing her name as if it were the most precious sound on earth.

"We've turned into a family," he whispered to her,

"and I want to keep it that way. We belong together, Katie. You know that as well as I do."

"Mark . . ."

"We belong together, right or wrong."

He drew Katie into his arms and held her.

It was wrong. Katie didn't need Mary Grace to tell her that Mark may have chosen her, but he hadn't chosen God. Her tears of joy quickly turned to tears of sorrow, and she pushed him firmly away.

"Katie?"

"We can't."

"Yes, we can. There isn't anything we can't work through together."

"Mark, you said 'right or wrong.' This *is* wrong."

He held her by the shoulders and searched her face. "This is real life, Katie. We can't let a few little differences ruin what we've found together."

"They're not little differences, Mark."

"Big differences, then. Lots of people manage to compromise and they're happy doing it—"

"I can't. I couldn't live such a double life."

"Who said it would be—"

"I do. I couldn't live with you and know I couldn't share the most important part of my life with you. We'd be unequally yoked and I can't do that. The center of my life would be separate from you."

"I'm asking you to marry me."

"I know!" she blurted, and her voice was ragged with despair. "But I can't do that, Mark. You've got to understand that."

Mark's eyes widened in disbelief. "Katie, we've just found each other. Don't throw it away."

"I'm sorry," she said heavily. "You've given me the same choice Steve did. It's either you or God. I can't be true to both of you."

"I wouldn't ask you to change anything. You can believe anything you want to. You can go to all the meetings and services you can find. It doesn't have to make any difference."

"It already does."

Mark swallowed hard. "I love you, Katie Reed," he said. "Don't do this to us."

Katie backed away from his touch and forced herself to walk away.

It was the hardest thing she had ever had to do. The pain of leaving Steve was forgotten in the agony of leaving Mark. She dared not look back for fear of failing. The brittle ground crunched under her feet and she was chilled all the way through. With all her heart she wanted to turn back.

CHAPTER 14

KATIE HEARD THE DAWN BEFORE she opened her eyes. Outside the tent a bird chirped tentatively, one twitter at a time, as if asking God's permission to begin the day. She sniffed the peculiar, moist smells of the mountain daybreak, and she slowly opened her eyes to the pale light filtering into the tent.

The last day.

She heard Mark moving around outside. His heavy boots crunched across the frosty ground and paused, only a few feet from where she was lying. His footsteps receded and she heard the clatter of wood as he dropped a load beside the campfire.

Laurie rolled over and stretched. Heather stirred and rubbed her cold little nose. Outside, the bird broke into energetic song.

Katie hesitated to move, trying to memorize the sensations. Each sight, sound, and fragrance seemed infinitely precious to her.

"Good morning," murmured Laurie.

"Hi!" chirped Heather.

Katie's heart ached when she thought of how much she would miss the girls.

Laurie was the first one out of the tent, eager to help

her father with the morning chores. She noticed at once that his tent was gone. "Hey! What happened?"

"I took it down. It's over there, by my pack." Mark gestured toward his khaki backpack, now filled with their survival gear. "We're leaving today."

Katie winced when she heard him say it, but Heather gasped and turned to her with joy lighting up her face. "Did you hear that? We're going home today!"

"I heard him," she said, and impulsively stroked Heather's cheek. "But we won't get home in one day, Heather. We may have to walk for three or four days before we find a town."

Heather didn't seem to hear her. "I'm going to tell Grandma about my fish! And I'm going to tell her about the bear and the mountain lion and the Bible stories and . . . and . . . all about you, too!"

Mark didn't look up when Katie came out of the tent. He used the spatula to nudge the fried perch out of the skillet onto the tin plates and immediately dunked the pan into the bucket to soak. Laurie handed Katie her plate. "Dad says we're going to walk out."

"It's great," piped Heather. "I'm sick of eating fish for breakfast. I'm going to have Sugar Frosted Flakes as soon as we get to Grandma's."

"That sounds good," said Katie. "I think I will, too."

"Are you coming to Grandma's, too?"

"No, honey. I'll go to my own house."

"I want you to come to Grandma's. There's another room across the hall where you can sleep."

"I'll come and visit you sometimes."

"When?"

"Soon."

"I want you to live with us!"

"I can't do that, but I'll come and—"

Heather turned to Laurie. "I want Katie to live with us."

"I'm not going to Grandma's," said Laurie. "I'm going home with Dad."

Heather stared at her, her lower lip quivering. "What?"

163

Laurie looked up at Katie. "You'll come and visit us, too, won't you?"

"You can't do that!" shouted Heather. "Grandma won't let you!"

"We'll see about that," said Mark.

"Laurie!" Heather started to cry. "You don't want to go home with him! You don't have to! He can't make you!"

"I want to," said Laurie. "And if you want to know what I think, I think you should come home with us, too."

Heather jumped up and threw her plate on the ground. "I won't! I won't! I won't ever go home with him! I won't!" She broke into sobs and ran away from the campfire, heading toward the stream.

Katie went after her. "Heather! Heather, please wait!"

A huge black thing reared up in front of Heather.

Heather stopped dead and screamed.

There was no time to think. The bear was less than ten feet away. It swayed on its back legs, its immense forelegs pawing the air. Its black, beady eyes were fixed on Heather, and saliva dripped from its open, bawling mouth. Heather was paralyzed.

Katie heard shouting from behind her, but the roar of the beast drowned out the words. She grabbed Heather by the shoulders and spun her around, pushing her back toward the campfire. She caught a glimpse of Laurie and Mark, both on their feet, before she whirled around to face the bear again.

"Run!" shouted Mark. "Katie, run!"

The bear dropped to all fours and charged her. Katie ran. The foul musky odor overwhelmed her. She heard a gunshot and felt relieved for a second, until she realized the bear was still after her. Blindly she changed direction and ran toward the stream, toward the place where Laurie had been attacked weeks ago, attacked and chased and miraculously saved.

She heard Heather screaming at Mark to shoot and she wondered why he didn't, then remembered the day the

164

bear had come after Laurie. Mark had run after Laurie with his rifle, unable to fire for fear of hitting her, and Katie realized too late she had placed Mark in the same predicament. He couldn't risk hitting her. He couldn't shoot.

Her left foot slipped on the frost and she almost fell. She could hear the heaving breath of the bear as it gained on her. Ahead the promontory of rock jutted up and she raced toward it, hoping to find safety. Laurie had been saved there.

Her left foot slid on the slick grass. She lost her shoe and fell to her knees. The impact against the frozen ground sent streaks of sharp pain shooting up her thighs. She heard the bear grunting and she scrambled to her feet. She had to make it to the rocks.

The bear was on her. Its massive hot weight struck her and Katie hit the ground frontally, skinning the palms of her hands as she fell. She heard a second shot, then a third. She knew Mark had to be desperate to take the risk.

Three shots. Three. Now the clip would be empty. And the bear was still alive.

Claws spiked into her arms. The pressure on her back suffocated her and the musky smell was choking her, and she heard the fabric of her sweatshirt ripping. She tried to fight, but she was pinned flat to the ground beneath the bear. The pressure suddenly eased and Katie thought the bear was leaving, but it lifted her and flipped her over. She glimpsed yellowed teeth grinding above her, and she thrust her arms upward to protect her face. The massive jaws closed around her arm and clamped down, the teeth penetrating to the bone.

There had been no miracle. The bear was killing her.

She opened her mouth to cry out, but her throat constricted and no sound came out. She heard the rasping breathing of the bear in her ears and Mark's voice somewhere beyond it—no within. Her frightened mind called up the memory of his face, his deep hazel eyes fixed on her as he asked:

Why didn't you rebuke the bear? Haven't you heard those stories—

She felt her flesh tearing.

. . . and they just tell it to go away in . . .

"The name of Jesus!" she cried aloud. "Go away in the name of Jesus!"

Her arm thudded to the ground. The weight lifted from her chest. She gasped the cold air and felt it burn into her tortured lungs. She forced her eyes open and saw the bear running away from the rocks. Away from her.

A gunshot split the silence. The bear dropped and lay still.

Darkness overtook her. The last thing she heard was the astounded voice of Mark McLaren shouting, "That's impossible!"

Heather huddled at the foot of the sleeping bag, her eyes fastened on Katie's pale face. She watched her father touch Katie's wrist, counting the beats of her pulse. Laurie knelt beside her, across from Mark, her fingertips barely touching Katie's chestnut hair.

"Why doesn't she wake up?" asked Heather.

"She will. It takes time," said Laurie.

"It's been a long time already!"

Laurie licked her lips and looked at her father. "It's been six hours, Dad."

"I know what time it is."

"She's going to be all right, isn't she?"

"Of course she is!" Mark carefully unwrapped the bandage he had placed around Katie's arm, and removed the thick gauze padding. Laurie swallowed and trained the beam of the flashlight on the wound.

Even to her untrained eye, the infection was obvious.

"Can't you do anything else?" she asked.

"No."

"But it's getting worse!"

"She needs antibiotics. We don't have any."

"Can't it get better without them?"

Heather cuddled her doll and watched Mark's face, dreading the answer.

"Dad?" prodded Laurie.

Mark bit his lip and shook his head. Katie's arm was

166

red and swollen. It was worse than it had been thirty minutes ago. He had been a paramedic for fifteen years, but he had never seen an infection set in so quickly.

"What's going to happen to her, Dad?" asked Laurie.

"She's going to be all right."

"But you said she needed—"

Mark felt exhausted and defeated. Without the drugs she needed to fight the infection, Katie would grow steadily worse. Out here, without proper attention, her fever would rise and her entire body would become septic. There was no way to fight it off. Mark felt helpless, and he hated it. With all his years of training and experience, there was nothing he could do.

Nothing.

"She could die, couldn't she?" asked Laurie.

Mark nodded.

Heather clutched her princess doll and gaped at Mark. She watched him reach under the edge of the sleeping bag and pull the edge of the blue plaid blanket up over Katie's shoulders. She pointed at Katie's mouth. "Daddy," she said accusingly, "do it!"

Mark rubbed his tired eyes and examined the wound again.

"Daddy!"

"What? What did you say?"

"Do it!"

"Do what?"

"Kiss her alive!"

Mark stared at her, uncomprehending. Then Katie's words flashed through his mind and he realized what Heather meant.

"I can't do that, Heather."

"Yes, you can!"

"It won't do any good."

"Daddy!"

"Heather, listen to me." Mark put his hands on Heather's shaking shoulders. "Katie needs antibiotics. She needs to get to a doctor. I've done all I can. I can't help her."

"Yes, you can! Kiss her alive!" Heather's terrified

167

eyes blazed with anger. "You're going to kill her like Mommy!"

Mark tried to find the words to explain, but couldn't. He traced his fingertips over Katie's lips, then moved his hand to her forehead. He felt the heat of fever. Katie was getting worse by the minute.

"Daddy!"

Mark bent over and kissed Katie's lips.

Heather leaned forward expectantly.

There was no change. Katie's eyes remained closed. Her injured arm remained red and swollen. Heather stared at her, unbelieving.

Mark replaced the gauze and bandaged Katie's arm again. He placed it gently by her side.

Heather began to cry softly. The princess doll fell from her lap. The truth Katie had told her finally penetrated her heart.

"Daddy," she sobbed. "Oh, Daddy!"

She climbed into Mark's arms and clung to him.

Katie grew worse. Her face was flushed pink with fever, and her breathing became heavy and labored. Laurie bathed her face with cold water, trying to give her some kind of relief, but she could see from Mark's gray, haggard face that there was no help left they could give.

Mark put his tent back up and moved Heather into it. She protested sleepily, but exhaustion won the argument and she fell soundly asleep. Mark tucked her in lovingly, numb with overwhelming emotions. Heather had come back to him. Both of his daughters could love him again.

He wished Katie knew that. He tried to tell her, but he knew she couldn't hear.

He slept by her side, waking every few minutes to check her pulse and listen to her labored breathing. Laurie huddled in the corner of the tent, clinging to Katie's Bible, unable to rest until the approach of dawn.

The first light of morning had seeped into the tent. Mark raised up on his elbow and looked anxiously toward Katie.

She was twisting and tossing, still unconscious, and

wracked with fever. Mark knelt over her, trying to hold a cold compress against her forehead, but in delirium Katie fought him and writhed away.

Laurie sat up and felt Katie's Bible beneath her hand. She picked it up and held it close, as if she could absorb comfort through its leather binding.

"She can't die, Dad," she said suddenly. "Why would God let her die after she rebuked a bear in his name?"

"That's impossible," Mark whispered, his voice gravelly from exhaustion but still tinged with awe.

"We both saw it."

"Something else made it run away."

"What?"

"I don't know. Something."

"There wasn't anything else. It was God."

"That's impossible."

Mark suddenly handed Laurie the compress and left the tent. He had to be alone.

The morning was eerily quiet. Even the birds were silent. He walked toward the edge of camp, but his approach did not send little animals scurrying for cover as it usually did. For a moment he felt as if he were truly alone in the world. He hadn't felt that way since the night Adrian died.

The tail and empennage of the disabled plane swayed slightly in the morning breeze. Mark turned away from it and caught sight of the dead bear lying at the edge of the promontory.

"That's impossible," he said again.

But so was the sudden engine failure of the *Adrian*. So was the appearance of a flat, level strip of ground in the rugged terrain of the Montana Rockies. So was the landslide that had saved Laurie from the bear's first attack.

Mark breathed in deeply, thinking.

Finding Heather in the dark had been impossible.

Reconciling with Laurie had been impossible.

There was no conceivable way Katie could have found him after the deer gored him. She could not possibly have been guided by whistle blasts; he'd been too far away for her to have heard him.

And now, Heather loved him again.

He stared at the dead bear. If he didn't know better, he might begin to wonder if Katie Reed had been right about God.

"It doesn't make any sense," he said aloud. "If there is a plan, a purpose for all of this . . . then why is she dying?"

And then Mark understood.

He dropped to his knees on the frosty ground and gave up. He surrendered a year of bitterness and anguish. He lifted his wounded heart up to be healed. He shook with gratitude and sobbed out his thanks for the return of his daughters' love, and he marvelled at the depth of the love that had brought him out here to experience the impossible.

Peace enveloped his heart. He raised his tear-streaked face to the sky and prayed in faith for the life of Katie Reed.

When he rose to his feet he was dizzy with relief. He turned back toward the camp and took two steps before he heard the plane.

The mountains echoed with Mark's joyful shouts. He started to run, ignoring his aching leg, groping in his vest pocket for the lighter. He skidded the last few feet to the pyramid of wood and began to untie the tarp.

The sound of the engine grew louder. Mark abandoned the knots and reached for the bottle he had filled with fuel drained from the tanks of the plane. He doused the pyre and the tarp together, and flicked the lighter just as Laurie and Heather came running up to him. The fire caught, flames leaping toward the sky. Together they hurled the nearby tires on top of the pyre.

Black smoke rolled upward. Mark and his daughters waved their arms and jumped and shouted for good measure.

The plane circled over their heads and dipped its wings in greeting.

Within the hour, they were on their way home.

CHAPTER 15

KATIE WOKE TO THE AROMA of maple syrup, and stretched contentedly in Mark's warm sleeping bag. Pain shot through her arm and she groaned, blinking in the harsh, white light. The scent of syrup gave way to disinfectant, and the cozy sleeping bag faded into stark white sheets pulled crisply over the bed. She focused on an IV bottle, hung upside down and feeding into her good arm, and heard tinny music floating from a radio somewhere far away.

Katie realized with a jolt that she was no longer camped in the Montana Rockies.

Footsteps padded up and down in the corridor outside her room. Someone wheeled a heavy cart past, and an intercom called for a doctor she had never heard of. Katie squeezed her eyes shut and tried to remember what had happened, and where she was.

The bear.

Katie felt its hot breath blasting across her face and its massive paws crushing her into the rocky ground near the stream. She twisted and struggled, fighting to get away, hearing her own voice calling out to God and . . .

"Katie."

She stopped fighting at once. She heard a chair squeak

against the tile floor, and heard someone come up to the bed. She felt a warm, strong hand caress her hair and brush her cheek.

"Katie?"

She felt peace descend. "Mark."

"Who?"

Katie opened her eyes. The first thing she saw was the gold class ring with the brilliant red stone.

"It's me, Katie. It's Steve."

She felt dizzy and disoriented. "Steve—am I home?"

"Not yet. You're in a hospital close to Glacier Park."

"How long—?"

"Three days. You've been soaking up antibiotics and taking a very long time to wake up. You scared us all half to death!" He took both of her hands in his. "Especially me. When I found out what had happened—that your plane had gone down somewhere in the mountains—I thought my life was over! Nothing made sense to me anymore. We were so happy together, then suddenly you were gone. I'm never going to let that happen again. I'm not letting you out of my sight until we're back home and safely married."

Katie stared at him, uncomprehending. "Married?"

"Married, as in you and me. This time we're going to do it right. No more last minute fights and near-disasters. I've spent the last month of my life pacing the floor and going crazy. If I had any doubts about loving you—but I never did. I've got you back, and I'm never letting go of you again!"

"Oh, Steve . . . please, don't say that."

"I know, honey . . . you've been through an awful ordeal and you're tired and confused. I won't push you to make plans until you're back on your feet. But the minute you are—try fighting me off. Just try, manager." He bent his head and kissed her hands.

Katie struggled to form words. "Everything's changed."

"That's what I'm counting on."

Katie wished her head would clear. Thinking was an effort. There was no way she could possibly put into words what she was feeling. Her memories flowed and spilled together: the landing site, the landslide, finding Heather in the dark and Mark in the forest. She saw Mark and Laurie holding each other by the fire and heard the girl's halting prayer to come back to the Lord. Her memory of the bear attack was vivid and she knew without doubt that she had been miraculously saved.

She would never compromise her faith again.

"I can't do that, Steve," she whispered. "I can't be yoked unequally. . . ."

Steve's face hardened. "That's what she kept telling me, that friend of yours."

"Mary Grace."

"All the way up here, she kept saying that. I think that's where we went wrong before, Katie. You shouldn't let other people influence you so much."

"She's here?"

"And your mom and dad. They're downstairs getting coffee. They'll be back any minute, so I'm going to say this now. We belong together. It doesn't matter what anyone else thinks about it. . . ."

Katie winced as a stab of fresh pain coursed through her bandaged arm. Steve saw it and broke off. "I'm sorry. I said I wasn't going to push you, and I'm rushing things. We've got plenty of time to work this out later. Don't give up on me, Katie. I love you." He tightened his grip on her hands. "I promised your folks I'd have them paged if you woke up. I'd better do that."

"Steve, wait."

"What is it?" His face was hopeful.

"Where's Mark?"

Steve's eyes narrowed. "Mark?"

"Mark McLaren. He—"

"Oh, McLaren. The pilot who crashed you in the mountains."

"We didn't crash. We landed. He was always in control."

"If that's control, I'll take the train."

"Please, where is he? Where are the girls?"

"They're gone. I don't know where."

"Gone?"

"Gone."

Katie was flooded with disappointment. "Did he leave any messages for me?"

Steve played with her fingers and studied her face. "Is there anything about the last month of your life I should know about?"

Katie turned her head and scanned the top of her nightstand, searching for a note from Mark or his daughters. There was nothing but a water carafe, a plastic glass, and a vase of roses with Steve's name on the card.

"Did he say where he was going? Did he leave a number, or an address?" Katie felt dizzy and dropped her head back on the pillows.

Steve squeezed her hand so hard his ring dug into her fingers. "Is that what this is all about? Katie, did you go and fall in love with another man?"

Katie closed her eyes and swallowed. "Please, just tell me when he left."

Steve paused, and dropped her hand. "The day before yesterday, right after your folks and I arrived. He introduced himself to us, then two policemen walked out of the elevator and arrested him for kidnapping."

Steve left for Helena late that afternoon. Katie's father drove back with him, but her mother stayed on, sharing a hotel room with Mary Grace Kimball. They both spent most of the afternoon on the telephone, trying in vain to find out where Mark McLaren was being held, and what had become of his daughters.

"No one seems to know anything," said Mary Grace, maternally tucking in the edges of Katie's blanket. "My nephew's trying to find out what school the girls go to, so we can get an address and phone number for their grandmother. She may be able to fill us in on what's happening."

Katie groaned. "If only I'd asked them what her last name was! I don't have any idea where they've been living, or how to find out."

"They didn't vanish, Katie. Sooner or later we'll find them."

"But even if we do, their grandmother may not talk to us. Not if she thinks we want to help Mark." Katie closed her eyes and thought of the night Mark and Laurie had reconciled. "Oh Mary Grace, kidnapping's a serious charge! Mark could go to prison for years!"

"From what you've told me, the older girl will speak up for him."

"But Heather won't. She still hates him. She'll say anything her grandmother tells her to."

"Is she more powerful than God?" Mary Grace kissed her forehead. "Don't be frightened, Katie. Just keep praying. If anyone should know how well that works, it should be you."

Another day passed with no news.

"You must be angry with me for sending Steve away again," Katie said to her mother. "I know you've never understood what happened between us, and why I couldn't go through with the wedding."

Katie's mother exchanged a glance with Mary Grace and smiled. "Oh, I don't know. I've spent a lot of time with Mary Grace in the last four weeks, and I've been learning a lot of things I never knew before. When all this is over and you're home again, I've got some questions to ask you about your faith."

"See? Something good came out of all this," said Mary Grace.

Katie was touched and grateful, but she was still confused.

"God didn't send me out there with Mark and the girls just to get my mother's attention," she told Mary Grace the next morning. "Why would he do such a wonderful work with Laurie's heart, and then tear her and her father apart again?"

"He knows what he's doing," said Mary Grace, "but do you? It sounds to me like you've been trying on unequal yokes again. What will you do when you find Mark McLaren?"

Katie hugged her Bible close to her. Mark must have

left it for her. "Nothing. I'm going to do nothing but trust God in all things."

But when Mary Grace left to meet her mother for lunch, Katie's resolve began to weaken. She let hot tears roll as she relived the pain of walking away from Mark McLaren and the girls she had come to love so much.

Rain tapped against the hospital window. She thought of the rain tapping on the tent and remembered telling Laurie, "Just make the decision. God will give you the feelings later."

Katie opened her Bible to Psalm 139. "I've made the decision, Lord," she whispered aloud. "And I'm trusting you to take care of my feelings, too. Please take the last month of my life and make the very best you can out of it. It's all yours, Lord. I give it up."

The peace that came over Katie's heart was past understanding.

Mary Grace pulled open the draperies and let the warm sunlight stream over the foot of Katie's bed. "Wake up, Katie," she called. "It's time to go down for your therapy."

Katie blinked at her, still drowsy. "Therapy? I'm not supposed to have therapy."

"Oh yes you are, and I don't know anyone who needs it more than you do." Mary Grace's eyes twinkled. "I've just had a long talk with your therapist, and I think you'll agree he's just what you've been looking for."

"What are you talking about?"

"Get up, dear. The wheelchair's here to take you to the lobby."

"The lobby? What's in the lobby?"

"My daughters," said Mark McLaren. "They're not old enough to visit you, so I'm taking you to visit them."

"Mark!" Katie sat upright, heart thudding. "Mark! What happened to you? Where have you been?"

Mark pushed the wheelchair up to the side of her bed. "I'll tell you when we get downstairs. I know better than to try to make my girls wait."

Mary Grace wrapped Katie in her robe and Mark gave

her his hand. It was like the first time they met, when Mark had helped her climb aboard a flimsy, blue and white airplane. Katie dropped into the wheelchair, slightly dizzy from spending five days in bed, and shivered with excitement as he pushed her out into the corridor.

"Mark! Please tell me what happened!"

"Before or after I got arrested?"

"After."

"I was fingerprinted and photographed with a number across my chest. I'll try to get you a copy to carry in your wallet."

"Mark, please! What happened?" Katie tried to twist around and see his face.

"I was taken to court for arraignment. My lawyer got about two words out before two crazy little girls thundered into the courtroom and turned the place upside down. They were both talking at once, telling the judge how they'd wanted to go with me and got on the plane of their own free will—you never heard such perjury in your life."

"They did? They said—? Both of them?"

Mark's voice caught. "The most important thing they said was that they loved me and wanted to come home with me. The judge was so shocked he didn't know what to do. We all ended up in his chambers, and Heather wound up on his lap, telling him about her fish. He finally threw it all out of court. We've been pigging out on Sugar Frosted Flakes ever since."

Katie was laughing and crying at the same time. "But what about Heather? She said she hated you!"

"That's all over now. We've got a long story to tell you, starting when you rebuked that bear and the Lord preserved your life. Then he touched Heather's heart with the truth and restored her love to me, and—oh, here they come."

"Katie! Katie!" Heather and Laurie jumped up off the couch in the lobby and swarmed around the wheelchair. Katie hugged them tightly, and stared up at Mark over their heads. She was amazed by how much younger he

177

looked, his face relaxed and free of tension and worry. Around his neck hung a simple silver cross. Katie saw it, and her heart filled with such joy she could hardly contain it.

Mark reached up and touched the cross. "While you were out, I came home."

Katie quivered all over. Heather bounced up and down in front of her. "We're getting a new house. Daddy sold the old one and we're all stuffed together in this awful apartment with no room for bikes, but we're getting a new house and a dog if we want one!"

"And we'll go camping and fishing in the spring when Dad's not on at the fire station," said Laurie. "Dad said after all the practice you had, you'd camp rings around us all!"

"What kind of dog do you want, Katie? And we're going to paint the house your favorite color. What's your favorite color?"

"What's your favorite kind of dog? We're going to get you a bike, too. What color do you want your bike to be?"

"Will you marry us?" asked Mark. "We'll never make you fly or eat fish."

Heather and Laurie stopped talking and knelt by the sides of the wheelchair, anxiously scanning Laurie's face, waiting for her answer.

"Gingersnaps at the wedding?" said Katie.

Katie was lifted out of her wheelchair and pulled across Mark's lap. Over his shoulder she saw Mary Grace Kimball giving her the thumbs-up sign.

And Mary Grace Kimball had always been right.

ABOUT THE AUTHOR

JAN SEABAUGH, an Ohio native, has written stories for a number of magazines. *The Wings of Adrian*, her first inspirational romance novel, has a twofold theme: "forgiveness/reconciliation" and "the personal interest and powerful intervention of God in the lives of his children."

Seabaugh lives in her home state with her pilot-camper husband. Together they minister the gospel to children, both in their church and out in the neighborhoods. They have two children of their own.

A Letter to Our Readers

Dear Reader:

Welcome to Serenade Books—a series designed to bring you beautiful love stories in the world of inspirational romance. They will uplift you, encourage you, and provide hours of wholesome entertainment, so thousands of readers have testified. That we might better contribute to your reading enjoyment, we would appreciate your taking a few minutes to respond to the following questions and return to:

> Lois Taylor
> Serenade Books
> The Zondervan Publishing House
> 1415 Lake Drive, S.E.
> Grand Rapids, Michigan 49506

1. Did you enjoy reading *The Wings of Adrian*?

   ☐ Very much. I would like to see more books by this author!
   ☐ Moderately
   ☐ I would have enjoyed it more if _____

2. Where did you purchase this book? _____

3. What influenced your decision to purchase this book?

   ☐ Cover   ☐ Back cover copy
   ☐ Title   ☐ Friends
   ☐ Publicity   ☐ Other _____

4. Please rate the following elements from 1 (poor) to 10 (superior).

☐ Heroine   ☐ Plot
☐ Hero   ☐ Inspirational theme
☐ Setting   ☐ Secondary characters

5. What are some inspirational themes you would like to see treated in future books?

_____

_____

6. Please indicate your age range:

☐ Under 18   ☐ 25–34   ☐ 46–55
☐ 18–24   ☐ 35–45   ☐ Over 55

Serenade / Saga books are inspirational romances in historical settings, designed to bring you a joyful, heart-lifting reading experience.

Serenade / Saga books available in your local bookstore:

#1 *Summer Snow*, Sandy Dengler
#2 *Call Her Blessed*, Jeanette Gilge
#3 *Ina*, Karen Baker Kletzing
#4 *Juliana of Clover Hill*, Brenda Knight Graham
#5 *Song of the Nereids*, Sandy Dengler
#6 *Anna's Rocking Chair*, Elaine Watson
#7 *In Love's Own Time*, Susan C. Feldhake
#8 *Yankee Bride*, Jane Peart
#9 *Light of My Heart*, Kathleen Karr
#10 *Love Beyond Surrender*, Susan C. Feldhake
#11 *All the Days After Sunday*, Jeanette Gilge
#12 *Winterspring*, Sandy Dengler
#13 *Hand Me Down the Dawn*,
    Mary Harwell Sayler
#14 *Rebel Bride*, Jane Peart
#15 *Speak Softly, Love*, Kathleen Yapp
#16 *From This Day Forward*, Kathleen Karr
#17 *The River Between*, Jacquelyn Cook
#18 *Valiant Bride*, Jane Peart
#19 *Wait for the Sun*, Maryn Langer
#20 *Kincaid of Cripple Creek*, Peggy Darty
#21 *Love's Gentle Journey*, Kay Cornelius
#22 *Applegate Landing*, Jean Conrad
#23 *Beyond the Smoky Curtain*,
    Mary Harwell Sayler
#24 *To Dwell in the Land*, Elaine Watson
#25 *Moon for a Candle*, Maryn Langer
#26 *The Conviction of Charlotte Grey*,
    Jeanne Cheyney
#27 *Opal Fire*, Sandy Dengler
#28 *Divide the Joy*, Maryn Langer
#29 *Cimarron Sunset*, Peggy Darty
#30 *This Rolling Land*, Sandy Dengler
#31 *The Wind Along the River*, Jacquelyn Cook

Serenade / Serenata books are inspirational romances in contemporary settings, designed to bring you a joyful, heart-lifting reading experience.

Serenade / Serenata books available in your local bookstore:

#1 *On Wings of Love*, Elaine L. Schulte
#2 *Love's Sweet Promise*, Susan C. Feldhake
#3 *For Love Alone*, Susan C. Feldhake
#4 *Love's Late Spring*, Lydia Heermann
#5 *In Comes Love*, Mab Graff Hoover
#6 *Fountain of Love*, Velma S. Daniels and Peggy E. King
#7 *Morning Song*, Linda Herring
#8 *A Mountain to Stand Strong*, Peggy Darty
#9 *Love's Perfect Image*, Judy Baer
#10 *Smoky Mountain Sunrise*, Yvonne Lehman
#11 *Greengold Autumn*, Donna Fletcher Crow
#12 *Irresistible Love*, Elaine Anne McAvoy
#13 *Eternal Flame*, Lurlene McDaniel
#14 *Windsong*, Linda Herring
#15 *Forever Eden*, Barbara Bennett
#16 *Call of the Dove*, Madge Harrah
#17 *The Desires of Your Heart*, Donna Fletcher Crow
#18 *Tender Adversary*, Judy Baer
#19 *Halfway to Heaven*, Nancy Johanson
#20 *Hold Fast the Dream*, Lurlene McDaniel
#21 *The Disguise of Love*, Mary LaPietra
#22 *Through a Glass Darkly*, Sara Mitchell
#23 *More Than a Summer's Love*, Yvonne Lehman
#24 *Language of the Heart*, Jeanne Anders
#25 *One More River*, Suzanne Pierson Ellison
#26 *Journey Toward Tomorrow*, Karyn Carr
#27 *Flower of the Sea*, Amanda Clark
#28 *Shadows Along the Ice*, Judy Baer
#29 *Born to Be One*, Cathie LeNoir
#30 *Heart Aflame*, Susan Kirby
#31 *By Love Restored*, Nancy Johanson

#32 *Karaleen*, Mary Carpenter Reid
#33 *Love's Full Circle*, Lurlene McDaniel
#34 *A New Love*, Mab Graff Hoover
#35 *The Lessons of Love*, Susan Phillips
#36 *For Always*, Molly Noble Bull
#37 *A Song in the Night*, Sara Mitchell
#38 *Love Unmerited*, Donna Fletcher Crow
#39 *Thetis Island*, Brenda Willoughby
#40 *Love More Precious*, Marilyn Austin

Watch for other books in both the *Serenade/Saga* (historical) and *Serenade/Serenata* (contemporary) series, coming soon.